GUTTA BOYZ

Bryan K. Johnson

Copyright 2014 © by: Bryan K. Johnson

Boot Publishing Inc.
14785 Preston Rd. Ste. 550
Dallas, TX 75254
Email address: bootpublishing@gmail.com

Visit us on our Web site @ www: bootpublishing.com

Editor: Shanara L. Hollins-Hawkins
Cover Design by: Dex Strattman

ISBN-13: 978-0692392676 (Boot Publishing)
ISBN-10: 069239267X

Library of Congress Control Number: 2015903945
Boot Publishing, Dallas, Texas

Published by:
Boot Publishing

Printed in the United States of America

DEDICATION

This book is dedicated to my future wife, Shamecko, who put her all into helping me get my book published. To my precious mother Terry, thank you for never missing a beat. To my dawg, my uncle, my Pops, or whoever I needed him to be, Valrice "Whop" Cooper, thank you for spending countless hours tapping on the typewriter as I told this story. To my "Teedy," Jacqueline, who made all this happen. I love you guys!

R.I.P

Darrilyn "Boosie" Johnson: 1988-1997
Margaret "Lil-Red" Johnson: 1957-2013
Shirley "Susie" Johnson: 1958-2005

DEDICATION

ACKNOWLEDGMENT

First, let me give thanks to my Lord and Savior because without him, I would not be where I am today. Thanks to my son Bryan who has traveled this road with me. Thanks to my step-daughters, Ty and Mira, and my mother-in-law, Gloria "Mama G" who never judged me for being in prison. Thanks to my brothers Eric "Baby-Face," Darryl "Po," and Robert "Rob" for the love they have given. Thanks to my cousin C-Mo and Derrick who always came thru. Thanks to my family who I can count on, especially my Aunt Mae who has also been there since I walked thru these gates. Thanks to my mother's fiancé, Wayne, who did not hesitate with the money to help me get my books copyrighted. Thanks to my homie Jam, and the rest of my homies who went home and kept it gutta wit cha boy--much love. Thanks to all the females who hold their men down while they are locked up because it's y'all that make it so much easier for a brother. Thanks to everyone who read my book when it was written in a spiral tablet and encouraged me to keep doing my thing. Anyone who I may have forgotten, don't trip. It's all gravy. Charge it to my head and not my heart. Last but not least, thanks to all of my fans. With lots of love.

ABOUT THE AUTHOR

June 2015, I was released from Dixon Correctional located in Jackson, LA after being incarcerated seventeen years and three months. Currently I resides at City of Faith in Monroe, LA. As of now I am strengenth my personal relationship with God as I allow him to direct my path. I am also determined to be a positive influence and the next big thing in this Urban World.

AUTOBIOGRAPHY

My name is Bryan Keith Johnson. I was born in January of 1982. I was raised by my mother Terry Johnson and my grandmother Carrie Mae "Bernard" Johnson in the small town of Plaquemine, Louisiana. I was the oldest of my mother's four children (Eric Johnson, Darryl Johnson, and Darrilyn Johnson). Growing up in a single parent home watching my mom try and raise four children with little to no help forced me to become the man of the house at a young age. I never really knew how it felt to have a father so I learned, from the streets, how to survive.

On July 27, 1997, my life changed at the young age of nine. My only sister was killed in a drastic car accident by a drunk driver. Something I still to this day struggle to cope with. With the pain of losing my baby sister, the hurt of being rejected and neglected by my father, I became angry, and I held a lot of anger inside. I became a person who I am not proud of.

At the age of sixteen, eight days after my 16th birthday, in January of 1998, I was convicted of man-slaughter and sentenced to twenty-five years where I would have to do

85% of that time. So, now I was leaving behind my mother, my brothers, and an unborn son.

One year later in January of 1999, at the age of fifteen, my brother was convicted of armed robbery and was sentenced to sixteen years in prison.

Sixteen years later, I have become a better person: a person that I am very proud of, a person that one day my son will be very proud of, a person who's striving to do greater things, not just for myself, but for my family. I still don't know how it feels to have that father's love, but I do promise to give my children the love that I wasn't given.

Despite a life of falling short of my own potential, I've always held on to my faith in God because without him it's no way possible that I would've or could've made it thus far.

PRELUDE

Power-Up and Boo were two dudes who grew up in the Southside of Baton Rouge. Learning how to hustle at a young age led them both to a life of sticking people up. Going to prison taught Power-Up a valuable lesson about friends and family. He went in as a juvenile and came out a grown man. Now, everybody is trying to figure out how Power-Up came straight home from prison to do big things that would unexpectedly cause some major beef with his old friend.

CHAPTER ONE

Growing up in Louisiana where slavery was still a factor in many ways, made it hard for a lot of black people, especially a single mother raising four kids and working on minimum wages. Power-Up grew up in Baton Rouge, the state capital of Louisiana, where it was always a hood thing "to be or not to be." Just south side of the state capital was one of the most vicious hoods in Baton Rouge because thugs weren't only beefing with other hoods but also amongst themselves.

South 17th and America Street was made up of a bunch of apartment complexes' called the Section-A tags projects because it was run just like that—the projects. Power-Up was just turning thirteen and things were getting harder by the days coming and going. Power-Up was also beginning to see how his mom was stressing herself out trying to take care of four kids and pay bills by herself.

One day Power-Up came home from school and saw his mom's car still parked in front of their section, which kind of spooked him. It was rare for Ann to miss a day from work unless she or one of her kids was really sick. Other than that, it was work, work, work. Power-Up used his key and entered the apartment. He was kind of nervous not hearing a sound. But also not forgetting, they were staying where people hustled, robbed, prostituted, steal, or do just about anything to satisfy themselves.

Power-Up walked into the living room and there was still no sound of life. He quickly ran to her room where she was lying down sleeping. Looking at her made Power-Up wonder why was she single. Even though she had four kids she still looked good and damn good too. He let out a breath of relief.

"Ma! Ma!" Power-Up called.

As soon as she rolled over, he could sense something was wrong. The way her eyes were puffed he could tell that she had been crying for a while.

"Ma, you sick? Why you ain't gone to work?" Power-Up asked with worry in his voice.

"Which one do you want me to answer first?" she answered. Last time I remembered, I was your Mama."

"I was just wondering. I know you barely miss work unless it's something bad," Power-Up said.

"I quit my job this morning," she responded.

"I thought you liked your job," Power-Up said staring at her in bewilderment.

"I did," she replied. But Keith, always remember, some people will try and use you for what you got. Always remember that. I'll just find another job. Now get that look off your face. We gonna make it."

As Power-Up slowly backed out of his mama's room, he realized he had so many questions to ask her that he didn't have answers to. And, he hated not knowing. Maybe it was time for him to make the decision he dreaded having to make he thought to himself. As he was passing back through the living room, he had already made up his mind that the hustling game would be his best bet.

Most everyone in the projects had some kind of hustle from selling plates of food, frozen cups, and variety of candies. Power-Up knew where to start. His best friend Kevin Jackson, who everybody called "Boo," didn't just hustle one way. He did whatever it took to make a dollar. Everyone in his family was hustlers, so you can say Boo was born in the game. Boo was also from the projects but his mom and dad had made enough to move out even though they just moved one street over. They lived on Brice Street in a three bedroom house.

Power-Up could never understand why people talked about how they loved the projects but always wanted to move out. He guessed once he got a little older, he'd see why people wanted out. It's not a place to raise kids because many of them either ended up getting killed or would wind up in prison. So, it was a must for most to get out as soon as they could. Maybe *that* was everyone's dream in the projects.

Boo was three-years older than Power-Up, but for the similar way in which they carried themselves, you would think they were both the same age. Power-Up was on the way to Boo's house, taking a short cut through other people's yards when he heard gun shots fired.

Now, growing up in the hood hearing gun shots was nothing new, so he thought nothing of 'em. Then, the unexpected happened a nigga came stumbling from the side one of the houses holding his stomach. Got damn, he thought! Power-Up knew right then that he picked the wrong day to take a shortcut.

The first thing that hit his mind was to run. This was the early 90's, and around here during this era, you were taught to mind your own business. But seeing that it was Baby Flea, who lived behind the projects in Big D's, forced Power-Up to run towards him in an attempt to help. Baby Flea must have been thinking that whoever shot him wasn't finished because he went into his pant pockets and pulled out a Ziploc bag full of crack cocaine. He handed it to Power-Up and then waved his bloody hand gesturing for him to go.

Power-Up ran, forgetting all about his trip to Boo's house. He ran straight home thinking whoever got Baby Flea, was gonna get him too.

That was the beginning of Power-Up's hustling game.

CHAPTER TWO

Power-Up had a nice-sized Ziploc bag full of all different types of shapes of crack. He didn't know how much it was worth or what they sold for, but he did know who knew all about it. He was so anxious to find Boo, but he could sense that it would be safer to stay inside for the rest of the day.

The next day, Power-Up skipped school to go holla at Boo. He knew Boo would be at home because he only went to school the first and last weeks of each month. Walking to Boo's house felt different today than any other day because of what happened yesterday. Word got out that a junkie had tried to rob Baby Flea and then shot him when he refused to give up what he had. Instead of the junkie following him to take what he had, he got spooked and ran off.

That's one thing about the hood—a mutha fucka will always find out how shit happened. Even if it's a made-up story, something would be said about the situation. Power-Up made it to Boo's house and as usual had to damn near break the glass out the window from knocking so hard.

"Who dat?" he heard a voice reply.

"It's Power-Up," he yelled back. Then he heard the sound of footsteps drawing near to the door.

"I'm coming, man."

Power-Up walked toward the back door as Boo unlocked it. Before Power-Up went into the house, he played with the pit bull puppy that Boo's family kept in the back yard. After a few minutes, he walked into the house only to find that Boo had gone back to sleep.

"Man, get up!" Power-Up hollered.

"Why you ain't at school, man?" Boo replied.

"I ain't felt like going," Power-Up responded.

"What I told you 'bout that shit?" Boo said with a boot on his face.

"Man, fuck you," Power-Up shot back at him. "Why you ain't go yo'self?"

"Lil nigga, like I always say, I'm grown," Boo stated.

"Yeah, whatever," Power-Up said.

"Man, you heard what happened to Baby Flea?" Boo asked rubbing his eyes.

"Yeah, I was on my way over here when that shit happened. That's why I didn't go to school because I needed to holla at cha," Power-Up said.

"Bout what?" Boo asked as he looked at his friend with a confused expression.

"You said whenever I was ready to start hustling, you would teach me," Power-Up stated.

"What kind of hustle you wanna do?" Boo asked.

"Sell drugs," Power-Up stated plainly.

"That shit too slow. I thought you was talking about robbing, stealing cars, thangs like that. You need money to buy some work," Boo said.

"So, if I come up with the money or the work, you gonna show me how to do the damn thang?" Power-Up asked.

"Nigga, ain't 'ya my lil brother?" Boo asked. Power Up nodded, affirmatively, in agreement.

"Well then, balla, when you ready. You chillin' here for now cause I'm 'bout to get some Z's."

Power-Up stood to his feet and pulled the Ziploc bag out his pants. "What about this?" He said as he shook the bag in front of Boo's face.

"What the fuck!" was all Boo could say once he realized what was in the bag.

Power-Up knew he was about to ask a million questions. He cut him off and told him the story of how he bumped into Baby Flea when he got shot.

"Damn, lil brotha!" Boo was becoming more excited about the situation. "You ready to do this shit, or you want me to sell it and just break you off?"

Power-Up looked at Boo then looked at what he held in his hands and said, "I wanna learn how to hustle, and I trust you to tell me what everything is worth. I'll give you half." For some reason Power-Up felt like Boo wanted to get over on him. He seemed just too damn anxious once he'd seen the work.

"Hand the shit here to me so I can see how much we got," Boo said.

"Man, slow down," Power-Up stated. Before he could hand Boo the bag, he'd already snatched the mutha fucka.

Boo came from a conniving ass family who was always scheming or plotting a way to get paid. His momma would host dinners and card games where she'd cut big in the games, most of the time. His daddy sold ten and twenty dollar sacks of weed or a single joint for $3 a stick. His older brother, Josh, made his hustle stealing cars, and his sister, who was two years older than Boo, became a dope man's bitch at the age of fifteen. The rest of the family always had their hands in something. Power-Up felt at ease around them because he felt they was about a come up.

With no hesitation, Boo explained what a dime to a twenty dollar bag was. As he talked, Power-Up wrote it all down. Everything. Altogether, Boo said the work was a total of five and a quarter ounces of crack cocaine. Power-Up told Boo to split the crack. Power-Up had seen how niggaz tripped out in the movie, *New Jack City*, behind crack, so this was a test to see where their friendship really stood.

Boo handed Power-Up one and a quarter ounce while he kept the other four ounces. Power-Up thought to himself: here I am being real with my boy and he short changes me. Power-Up didn't trip though because he had already took three ounces out before he came to Boo's house. Now, his only worry was what he was going to tell his momma when she asked where all of the money was coming from. He knew that when the time came, he'd have some lie to tell; but until then, it was get money time.

Boo wanted to take Power-Up out to the projects to show him how to make sales. It was still school hours and Power-Up's momma still didn't have a job. The only thing Power-Up could do now was wait for school to let out and then start his first day on the job. This new job, he knew, would either get him killed or send him straight to juvenile hall.

Boo got up and threw on some clothes, walking into the bathroom to take care his hygiene.

"Say, Power-Up, you can chill here till school lets out if ya want 'cause I'm 'bout to go get off this. You know I'll be in the projects, so you can find me there. I'll show you how to twerk this shit," Boo stated.

And twerk it Power-Up did.

CHAPTER THREE

Power-Up started doing his thang in the hustle game. He was never told money makes you feel like you're bigger than you are. Well, that's how he felt. Boo had hooked him up with a nigga to score from whenever he ran out. About the time Power-Up made fifteen, he was all the way out there in the game. He wasn't just selling crack, he was also robbing people, breaking into people houses, and stealing cars. You name it, he'd do it. Power-Up was turning out to be just like all the other hustlers in the projects—doing whatever it took to get that almighty dollar.

To make matters worse, Power-Up's momma was tripping out on him. Saying how he went from being her oldest baby to being some mad man. He stayed gone for days without her knowing whether or not he was dead or alive. This was the year. 1996. The year Power-Up's mind had turned towards buying his first car. It was a two-door Monte Carlo, which he'd planned to have fixed up for the summer; and, only two things would ever stop him from getting his car: prison or death.

Power-Up was a few months from his sixteenth birthday, and it was time for him to start driving his own shit instead of rockin' renters. Besides, this lil hoe Power-Up was fuckin already said her crack head ass momma would put the car in her name. All Power-Up had to do was break her off.

By the time his sixteenth birthday rolled around, he'd gotten that car, and it had become to him what the hustling game was all about. Plus, it was a show piece—a symbol— of a young nigga doing his thang. His car had become his house on the streets. He slept in it. He fucked in it. He did everything in it. It was his pride behind wheels.

In between time, Boo had been staking out this jewelry store. He was sure that if they could hit that, it would put them on top of the game. Big time. He was talking twenty to thirty thousand dollars cash with boo coo of jewelry to sell on the streets. The jewelry itself was another twenty to thirty thousand dollars. Could they really be successful with a jewelry store heist? That kind of hit had Power-Up's mind racing like a race horse as he tried to figure it out.

Truth be told, the hustling game could not be any better than it already was for Power-Up. He had it all: girls, cars, money, jewelry, and J's. What more could he ask for, he thought?

Just then, his pager went off, bringing him out the daze he was thinking of his good fortune. He was lying next to one of his finest chicks. She was twenty-years-old with a fire-cracker mouth: always jealous as hell at everything or anyone that moved near him. She always wanted to know who was paging him and why, where the fuck he was going, who the hell he'd been with. All of her insecurities made Power-Up think she might be more worried about whether he was gonna find another hoe and do for that hoe what he was doing for her—paying all of her bills so she could keep her check from work and use it to get her hair and nails fixed every fuckin week. Not to mention, all of the designer clothes and shoes she was buying on a daily basis. Bitch thought she really had Power-Up's mind on love. But the truth to the matter was that he only put up with her because he didn't have to deal with his momma trippin on him at the crib. Plus, the girl was fuckin him to exhaustion, and what man would give that up?

Before Power-Up could pick up the phone to call his dude, there she was with her fire-cracker mouth, questioning him.

"Who that is?" she asked with disdain.

"Why?" Power-Up replied.

"That better not be no hoe! Let me see!" as she tried to get closer to the phone.

"Chill out. That's just Boo paging me, oh silly guh," Power-Up stated.

"Oh," she responded. "Baby, you know I love you. This dick for only me right?"

Power-Up ignored her, and started calling Boo back to see what was up as she started to unzip his pants and began to lick his dick like it was an ice cream cone.

"Hello?" Boo answered on the other end.

"What's up, Boo? It's me." Power-Up said.

"Laying back chillin," Boo said. "Everything is ready, and I'll pick you up at seven o'clock in the morning. That's what's up. Be ready," he concluded.

"Dawg I will, fa show," Power-Up replied.

"One" Boo said.

"One," Power-Up stated back then hung up the phone.

Power-Up fucked ole girl, Chasity, and put her to sleep so he could think about tomorrow. This wasn't no easy shit. This would be his first time robbing a business, so he had mad butterflies making his stomach queasy already. Taking a chance like that meant he needed to get his mind right, quick. Get what the fuck I want and get the fuck out, he thought. He fell asleep with that thought on his mind.

"Freeze mother-fuckers! Don't move, or I'll blow yo' dick in the dirt!" Power-Up and Chasity had been unexpectedly awoken from their nap. Naked and afraid, Chastity struggled trying to cover herself up.

"Didn't I say don't move! Now put y'all hands on y'all damn heads!"

"What the fuck you bitches want?" Power-Up heard himself boldly ask. Wasn't nobody gonna make him feel like no bitch in front of his hoe.

"We got a warrant for your arrest on second degree murder," the cop stated. "And you, nasty bitch, the officer said pointing at Chasity in disgust, for carnal knowledge of a juvenile."

Power-Up's survival instincts took over as he punched the white detective in his mouth. Blood came spewing from the cop's mouth, and then all hell broke loose. The mutha fuckas started beating Power-Up like he was Kunta Kinte from the movie Roots. He could feel himself going unconscious from the beating. The last thing he remembered hearing, was the muffled, blood curdling sound of Chasity screaming the word NO!

"Baby, wake up. Somebody knocking. You was having a bad dream," Chasity said. Power-Up looked over at her and gave her a kiss. He was so relieved that it was all just a dream. He looked at the clock—7:20a.m. Boo was already knocking at the door and from the sound of his knock, he was ready to go get paid.

Power-Up let him in the door, and then went took a shower not knowing it would be the last day that he and Boo would ever be friends. Boo had rented a '95 Maxima rock-renter. The plan was to use it to hit the lick, and then ditch it a few blocks over where another rock-renter would be parked.

They left Chasity's a few moments later, and as they were nearing the spot, Power-Up couldn't shake that uneasy feeling he had felt the night before. In that moment, he wished that he was still at home with Chasity, or just chillin on the block. Shit, anywhere but here. There was no turning back. There was no turning back now.

When they arrived at the spot, Power-Up parked the renter and jumped in the Maxima with Boo. He lit up a blunt, still nervous as an amateur nigga 'bout to fight Mike Tyson. He was hoping the blunt would help ease his mind a bit and take some of the edge off. Boo's calm demeanor did make Power-Up relax a little, but he re-checked his nine to make sure one was in the chamber.

The jewelry store opened at eight o' clock and it was now 8:10am. They pulled the renter to the side, placed their ski masks over their faces, gave each other pound, and jumped out the car with guns in hand.

The employees in the place never saw them coming until the bell on the door gave them away, but it was too late. Boo pointed his gun at the two behind the counter.

"Don't fuckin move!" he shouted. The woman stifled the scream with her hand over her mouth. "Where's the other one at?" he demanded, pointing the gun towards her face, but she was too afraid to respond. "Is y'all fuckin deaf?" Boo said in a threatening voice. He grabbed the white man and pointed his forty-five to his head. "Now I'ma ask one more time, where is the other one?"

The white woman pointed to a door leading towards the back office.

"Watch these two, and if they try something, just kill em," Boo said as he rushed towards the back office.

Power-Up nodded and was left standing there. He wondered why the fuck they didn't just get the shit that was already in sight. Boo disappeared for what felt like hours and came back with an old white man who looked like the kind who hated black folks. Then the unexpected happened. The younger white man tried to be a hero, and grabbed Power-Up. A struggle ensued between the two of them across the floor, and as they were tussling Boo shot the damned man in the back. The woman started screaming like crazy. This was not part of the plan. They could hear the sirens outside getting closer, and the look on Boo's face was one of extreme paranoia.

"Let's roll, Keith," he whispered out loud.

"Man, let's get some jewelry first," Power-Up replied. "I ain't do all this shit here for nothing!"

"We don't have time!" Boo hollered.

"Fuck that!" Power-Up shot back as he moved to where the watches were. He smashed the glass with his gun, and grabbed two armfuls of watches—as many watches as he could. Power-Up turned around towards where Boo had been standing, but Boo was gone. Frantically, he dashed out the door, and ran straight into the police—all with their guns drawn and aimed at him. He looked around for his friend, Boo. He was nowhere in sight.

"Freeze!!! Drop your weapon!" The police yelled from the bull-horn. At first thought, Power-Up wanted to shoot it out, but he thought twice, dropped his weapon and got on the ground as he'd been ordered. In an instant the policemen's behavior changed as they attacked him like a bunch of hyenas. They rushed and swarmed around him, placing the handcuffs around his wrists, jerking him up off the pavement, and then slamming his head on the hood of one of the police cars. Power-Up felt his brains rattle inside his head. He felt one of the racist pigs yank the ski mask off and ruff him up a little more before being thrown in the back seat.

From inside the back seat of the police car, Power-Up continued to look around for his friend. They must've already taken his friend in custody, he thought Slowly, he let his head sink down to his chest. He couldn't bear the shame of allowing someone in the streets to see him. His next thought was of his momma. He felt his body slumping lower forward.

A black policeman jumped behind the wheels of the police car and drove off. "Son, how old are you?" he asked. But Power-Up just sat there with a "fuck the world" look on his face and didn't have no rap for this cop ass nigga.

"Oh, you mad now?" he began saying. "That's what's wrong now with young punk ass niggaz. Y'all fucked up in life and wanna be mad at the world. Ain't nobody told you to come mess with these nice white folks shit."

"Man fuck you!" Power-Up screamed as anger began to quickly build inside him.

"Now, don't drop the soap or it's gonna be fuck you! The cop laughed menacingly. Get ready to start calling Louisiana State Penitentiary your home for the next thirty years. There's only one good came out this son, that man who was shot gonna make it out alright," the black cop stated.

The drive towards the police Head Quarter's gave Power-Up a long time to think about what went wrong, but he could not come up with the answers. The black cop was still running his mouth, making it hard for Power-Up to gather his thoughts.

"Son, next time you think about doing something like that again at least make sure no one sees you."

"What ya' mean by that?" Power-Up responded. He wanted to know who the fuck had seen them like that.

"Oh, you can talk? Maybe you can tell me who your friend was?" the cop questioned.

"What friend?" Power-Up replied. He could see the cop looking at him through the rear-view mirror.

"The fuckin guy that was with you, that's what fuckin friend," the cop said. Power-Up felt his back hit the seat. He could feel himself going into a state of mental shock. It couldn't be real. How the hell did Boo get away?

When he snapped back to reality, he could see from the police car window that they had made it to the headquarters.

He was placed in a room with mirrors everywhere. The room was small, with stark white ceilings, and freezing cold. About 45 minutes later, an old white man walked into the room. He looked to be somewhere in his late sixties. Right behind him, there followed a younger white male who read Power-Up his rights. Then, they started the interrogation. The first order of business was trying to get Power-Up to snitch on the friend who was with him during the robbery. Once they found out that he was only sixteen years old, they called his momma, and worked even harder attempting to convince her to get him to confess the name of his friend, but Power-Up was deep in the game now and there was no turning back. He, his mom, and the two detectives were just sitting there looking stupid when his mom made a request: "can I have a minute alone with my son?"

"Yes ma'am," the older detective replied. The younger, seemingly less experienced, detective was playing the "bad guy" role, acting like he didn't want to leave.

"Let's go, Juneshoro. Give her time with her son," the older one said.

Reluctantly, Juneshoro agreed, and when the door closed behind them, Power-Up's momma laid it all out.

"Keith, what have you done?" she demanded, staring Power-Up straight in the eyes as if she knew the answers were right there. "From the looks of things, they got you. That leaves you with two options. One, tell who was with you and get a lesser sentence since you wasn't the trigger man. Two, keep your mouth shut, and do the time for you and your boy, who left your ass out to rot. It's up to you. Whatever choice you make, I'm behind you 100%.

Power-Up thought about it for a moment. He knew what to do. His mom alerted the detectives that he was ready to talk.

The detectives walked back in with grins on their faces as if they knew what Power-Up was about to say. "You ready,

Mr. Keith?" the young detective asked. "This is a good choice you're making," he continued.

"I ain't said I was making no statement. In fact, I don't feel like talking," Power-Up stated in a defiant manner.

Detective Juneshoro got right up in Power-Up's face and began spit-screaming at him about how he was gonna rot in prison behind somebody who don't give a shit about him. The other, older detective, Starbuck, kept his cool throughout the entire ordeal. He asked Power-Up if it would be okay if they let him think for a few days and come to pay him a visit in a few days. PowerUp shook his head in agreement. In his mind, he didn't have any other choice at the moment. He kissed his mother on the cheek good-bye.

They booked him on attempted-first-degree murder and armed robbery. He was hauled off to the juvenile detention center. A few days later just as they'd discussed, the two detectives paid him a visit. The result they got this time was no different.

Power-Up lay in his jail cell and thought about the thirty to forty years that he was promised—either that, or the possibility of a juvenile sentence allowing him to release upon his 21st birthday if he snitched. Every day, Chasity stayed on his mind. It was strange, but Power-Up even felt like he really loved her. He knew that in the end, the hood motto would always be "death before dishonor." Would she wait for him on the outside while he did his time?

The judge sentenced him to ten-years in prison, with the promise of release in 8.5 on good behavior.

That was way back at the beginning of his "jose." He was lucky that the older prisoners looked out for him since he was just a young buck. They pulled for him to get in 8.5 on good behavior, so he could get his life back while he was still young enough to do so. Throughout the entire 8.5 years, he lost family members and friends to drugs and murder, and life. So many people forget about you after you've been on the inside for a while. That was, he knew, just a harsh reality of prison life. He also gained a lot, too—a dude that became like a big brother to him, his ace. He had been there from the time he got in, and Power-Up knew that he would be there for him at the time when he got out, and that moment had come. In two hours, Power-Up would become a free man.

CHAPTER FOUR

Life After Prison

Power-Up was finally freed after serving eight years and ten months in prison, which seemed like forever at first. The lack of communication with the outside world seemed to make the time move so slowly. His so-called girl, Chasity, never once hollered at him throughout his whole jose in prison. Not even his best friend, Boo. The nigga who Power-Up kept it gutta with acted like he never knew who he was. In fact, one time his mom said when she had seen him a few times; he would act like he didn't see her or just turn and go the other way.

Even some of his family members never once asked how he was doing. It was a good thing that he had a mama that stuck by his side cause it woulda been a lot harder doing that time. The last thirty months went by really smooth, which really meant that he had to just make the best out of a bad situation. It really is true that while you doing time in prison you actually live among enemies every day, but when you find a real friend in prison, you have found a real friend for life. That's how Tyree Smith aka "Jam" and Power-Up became best friends. When shit wasn't adding up on the outside, it was Jam that held Power-Up down when he was hurting in the can. As the time neared for Jam's release date, they were kicking it every day about plans to keep it real with one another hundred-times over. When Jam finally parted ways with Power-Up in prison he had nineteen months left.

In prison you would really never know a nigga is a man of his word until after he's out and stands by his word. Not that Power-Up had any reasons to doubt Jam's word, but it was just the way shit was. Jam went beyond keeping his word with Power-Up, though.

Jam was seven years older than Power-Up, and he always called him his lil brother. Dude was no bragger, but Jam used to stress to Power-Up how he gonna put him all the way in the game. Jam used to say that he was already straight, but when Power-Up nineteen months was up, with Jam in his corner on the outside, he would have much more. The flicks he was sending Power-Up over the months was evident that he was doing his thang. Classic cars that were hot shit to look at no matter what your taste in cars was. Not to mention all the fine ass bitches surrounding him on every damn flick he sent.

But, Power-Up kinda knew the nigga was official based on how he used to live in the can. Prison is somewhat like the streets on the survival level because mostly everybody in prison did some type of hustling. Jam was the weed man. That's how he and Power-Up became cool.

One day, Power-Up was hurting to get high and he asked Jam to credit him a joint until he got straight. Jam was like, "nah I'll do better, take these two and that's on me."

Knowing prison wasn't based on giving a nigga shit, Power-Up knew instinctively that he would return the favor, and he told Jam so.

"Man, look I ain't playing games. You a soldier. I wouldn't disrespect you like that," Jam replied.

From that moment on Jam and Power-Up built a solid relationship. Jam introduced Power-Up to his family over the phone and sometimes they'd visit at the same time. One time, they went visited together and Power-Up took one look at Jam sister Nakeba Smith and was like dammmmn!! Power-Up swore that one day, she was going to be all his. Jam always stressed to him though that Keba was off limits to him and he should treat her like a sister. That shit statement went in one ear and out the other. Power-Up was in love at first sight.

Power-Up had been back on the streets for five months now, and the world moved so fast for what he could recall about it before he went in the can. It felt like he had been out on the streets for five years seeing how fast shit going for him. He had a few places on lock already, and wouldn't stop until he had a lot more.

Ring! Rinng! Rinng! Power-Up's cell phone went off. He still hadn't gotten used to how the cell phones be ringing the way they do, anytime and anywhere.

"What's up," Power-Up answered.

"What's up Power-Up? You still gonna chill at the sports bar?" the caller asked.

"Yeah," Power-Up said realizing it was Jam on the other end. I'll meet you there."

"Cool. I gotta catch up with Young-One and A-k. We going round there at seven o'clock," Jam stated.

"One," Power-Up said.

"One," Jam responded.

It was a Sunday on Gus Young at the Super Sunday, some shit went down. Super Sunday was mostly where everybody who doing it big or thought they were doing it big came out and just hung out doing whatever. Like some shit you'd see on Crewshaw in the movie *Boyz-n-the Hood*. Being from Gardere Lane, Young-One and A-K got into some shit with some niggaz from Parktown. Super Sunday is located in Parktown so they were outnumbered. Luckily, they were strapped and ready for whatever.

Jam, not wanting to see anybody get murdered behind bullshit, talked the niggaz from the Park into chillin. The only reason blood was spared and nothing went down was because of the respect a lot of niggaz had for Jam.

From that incident on, Jam made them two lil niggaz his soldiers. A-K was a young nigga who'd shoot first and deal with everything else later, while Young-One would act a fool and put that tool on you only if he was being cornered. A-K was a heartless nigga being that both of his brothers was doing life sentences in the Louisiana State Penitentiary for murder and armed robbery. He saw his mother, whom he loved so much, drank herself to death at the age of 34 years old. That left his grandmother to raise him, and even though she loved her youngest grandson, he still felt like he was alone in this cold world.

Young-One, on the other hand, was a cool nigga until you crossed him the wrong way. Young-One and A-K looked out for each other coming from similar paths. Young-One's only sister was a dope-man's-bitch and his mom did anything to get high off the crack pipe. He and A-K felt like brothers because neither of them knew their fathers. And since meeting Jam, life seemed to be much easier making money and fuckin a lot of women while riding around in up-to-date whips along with their own cribs.

Power-Up didn't play too many clubs, but the sports bar was a laid back environment where you just drank, listened to music, shoot pool or dice, or watch women shake their asses. Power-Up spotted Jam as he walked through the door chillin while sippin on some Hennessey and coke chatting it up with a female who had an ass like Serena Williams. He spotted Power-Up and raised his drink in the air. He made his way over to where Jam was.

"What's up," Power-Up said when he walked up. "Ain't much," Jam replied.

"Who dis?" Power-Up asked him referring to the female.

"I have never seen her before."

"This Sugar Doo."

"Sugar, this is my brother, Power-Up," Jam said introducing him and the girl.

"How you get a name like that?" Power-Up asked the sweet looking thang.

She looked Power-Up up and down before she responded, "cause I'm sweet like sugar and I'll do whatever" Instantly Power-Up wanted to fuck her on the spot but knowing Jam was going to fuck her lights out made him back up. I'll catch Sugar Doo at another time he thought to himself.

A-K came bouncing through the door like he owned the place with that devilish grin on his face. Once YoungOne made it, they did the usual, and shot some partners pool. It was Power-Up and A-K against Jam and YoungOne. They talked about how everything was coming along with all the spots. So far everything was flowing well. It was time to re-up shit.

Jam and YoungOne was kicking Power-Up and A-K ass by six to two. A-K was mad as hell because he hated for YoungOne to beat him in anything. Power-Up was trying to scope out some pussy to leave with, when he and A-K started fussing.

"Fuck you! I'm going talk to that sexy lady with the red apple bottoms on with that loose booty," Power-Up told A-K.

"That's why we lost cause you been watching that hoe all night," A-K said.

"She's been watching me too," Power-Up told A-K, laughing.

"How you know she wasn't watching one of us?" A-K questioned.

"Fuck you, I'm out," Power-Up said as he walked off leaving A-K with the stupid boot on his face.

Jam and YoungOne was listening in and laughing their asses off at the shenanigans. Power-Up made his way over to the girl with the apple bottoms on. The DJ was right on time when he started playing that Lil Boosie's 'booty talk'. Apple bottoms grabbed Power-Up's hand and pulled him on the dance floor before he could say a word. She was making that booty talk on Power-Up's dick. The first thing Power-Up asked her was, "are you leaving with me?"

"I have my own car," Apple Bottom responded, confidently.

"How about you follow me?" She shook her head yes and smiled. The song went off, and Power-Up asked her if she was ready to leave. She was. Power-Up went to find Jam, who was still talking with Sugar Doo, gave him dap, and let him know he was leaving. Power-Up hollered at YoungOne and A-K who were still beefing on the pool table. Then, he left the building to go have a good time with Apple Bottoms. He wondered what her real name was.

Being that Power-Up didn't bring too many women to his crib unless he considered them special, he instructed her to follow him to the Holiday Inn Hotel.

After checking in and getting the keys to room #207, they exited the lobby to head upstairs to the room. On the way to room #207, Power-Up was squeezing every part of her body. It took them at least ten minutes to make it inside. All Power-Up kept thinking was he wish her pussy smelled good because he wanted to taste it. Soon as the door shut he started undressing her, quickly, until she was in her birthday suit. Power-Up started sucking on her neck while rubbing on her pussy. He moved to her titties, which was the perfect size for him—not too big and not too small. He nibbled on both of them and moved down to her flat stomach. She couldn't have had any kids with a stomach like that, he thought. By this time Power-Up had his middle finger inside her love nest which was wetter than a river fall on a hot summer day.

On his way down Power-Up switched fingers and smelled the one he had inside and yes it smelled sweet. He attacked her clit with his tongue, inserted another finger in her and that did it.

"Ohh, right there baby! That feeel sooo goood! Ahhhh! I'm bout to, ahhhh. Shit! I'm commmming! Aaaahhh! MMmmmmmm."

Power-Up stood up, still fully clothed, and stuck his tongue in her mouth.

"Taste your pussy; don't it taste good?" he whispered in her ear. She responded by sticking her tongue further into his mouth. "Mmmmmm."

Power-Up knew his dick was ready to go to work from the way it was trying to bust out his pants. She kneeled before him and started to pull his pants down. She had his dick in her hands and began to place small licks and kisses on it. Then Power-Up felt her place him into her mouth and started sucking him like his dick was an ice cream cone.

After their mad oral sex they spent the rest of the evening fucking each other as if the world was going to end the next day. Power-Up didn't remember which one of them dozed off first but being in prison he collected the habit of waking up early. She was still asleep when he went to the bathroom to wash up. Her body was so beautiful and sexy laying there in the hotel bed. He wrote her a little note before he left because he felt that she might be worth keeping in contact. Yes, it was a definite must to keep her on the menu to eat some more, he thought as he glanced at her once more. Then he began write:

Sorry I don't know your name, but you don't know mine either. Just wanted to let you know I had a good time. If you felt the same, hit me up on my cell number: 302-2735. Name is PowerUp, and I'll just call you Apple Bottoms.

CHAPTER FIVE

A-K had always been considered a bad boy who never gave a fuck bout anything, except for his family and best friend YoungOne, until he met Jam and Power-Up. A lot of people in the hood knew him but once he hooked up with the likes of Jam and Power-Up, he had become known throughout Baton Rouge and the surrounding areas.

A-K was just like Power-Up and YoungOne, making more money than a mutha fucka working ten jobs would ever see in a damn lifetime. In spite of that, he always managed to end up in some bum shit. Money, power, and respect: he had it all. What else could anyone ask for?

Two days had passed since they were all together even though they talked to each other every day over the cells. It was Thursday evening, and A-K was cruising through one of the hoods called Dixie in his all white Dodge Magnum sitting on 24s with his 12s beating down the block, when, three dudes sitting in a Cadillac CTS were blocking his path while talking to some females.

A-K started blowing his horn and even sticking his arm out the window gesturing for the niggaz to move so he can pass. The driver of the car was about to move his car when the nigga on the passenger side jumped out talking shit. A-K guessed he was trying to impress the women they was getting at even though he knew who A-K was. There's always somebody that don't care who you are and will try to get stripes off you.

Dude got out the car and started walking up on A-K's car still talking shit when A-K jumped out his car and shot him twice, one time in the chest and one time in the arm. A-K then jumped back into his ride and drove outta there as soon as possible.

It was early evening the next day when Power-Up, Jam, and YoungOne was sitting in the parish jail's parking lot waiting on A-K to come out. They had sent bail money to the bonds man in the amount of two hundred thousand dollars to get him released on bond.

"There's that fool right there," YoungOne said after spotting A-K.

Jam's money-green Tahoe sitting on 26's was parked in the center of the parking lot. Soon as A-K got inside the Tahoe, Jam started his attack.

"What's the fuck wrong withcha A-K?" Jam asked with anger in his voice.

"Whatcha mean?" A-K shot back, but he knew what was coming.

"Man, I'm trying to make 'ya rich before 'ya 25 years old not see 'ya with life before 25," Jam explained.

"That fool disrespected me," A-K said.

"I always tell 'ya small things 'ya gotta let slide. These niggaz know who ya are and what ya'll do to them." Jam looked at A-K seriously then concluded, "I won't let nobody disrespect me either, but we are niggaz getting money. Never let something stupid stop that from happening."

A-K hated when Jam talked crazy to him, but he felt Jam was right about what he was telling him, so he said nothing else. Everything was quiet for a few minutes until A-K broke the silence.

"Dawg, ya right. I won't let something small stop me from getting my cake up," A-K expressed. They all started giving A-K pound and cracking jokes on him about jail.

"Where's the fuckin purple at?" YoungOne asked.

"Damn, that's all ya wanna do is smoke blunts," Jam said.

"Look who's talkin," Power-Up said. "Man, let's swing by Keba's Beauty Salon on the way back."

Keba's Beauty Salon was Jam's sister's shop. Keba stood bout 5'6 at 127 pounds with a nice ass. It was not too big and not too small, just like Power-Up liked it. She had a smooth dark complexion with the perfect size titties. She always wore her hair hanging long and loose. Power-Up had a serious hidden crush on her and swore she was made perfect for him only. There was, of course, one major problem with Power-Up's secret crush on Keba—Jam. As his boy, and big brother, he had expressed that his sister Keba was off limits to the crew.

They pulled up in front of the shop and Power-Up immediately started looking for Keba. He couldn't help himself. His attraction to her was instinctive. People always say that the church is the place to find a woman, but on the flip side, Power-Up thought, Keba's Beauty Salon was the place to find the women because it stayed packed with bitches six days a week from sun up to sundown. They all stepped out the truck with enough bling on their necks, wrists, and fingers to blind a blind person.

As soon as they hit the door all that could be heard was a clamor of voices saying, "Aahhh, there they go!"

Jam asked one of the girls, Mini, who worked at one of the chairs where Keba was.

"She's in her office," Mini said licking her lips at the same time. Mini stood around 5'7 at about 145 pounds with a nice shape on her, too. Then, there was the one they called Chocolate Thunda who had the sexiest lips you could imagine her ass was quite bodacious, too. Yoshi, another woman who worked at the shop, stood at 5'8 at about 135 pounds, but she didn't have too much ass on her at all. Even still, she had it going on, and she was sexy as all out doors. The one whom they called Meech was 5'5 and about 130 pounds. She was kinda on the thick side with no body fat—just everything on her body all in the right places.

"Damn, A-K, I hear you still shooting niggaz like it's a hobby, huh?" Mini said.

"Mind your own fuckin business," A-K shot back quickly.

"If you act like you got some sense, I wouldn't know ya business," Mini replied.

"Fuck you," was the only comeback A-K could muster.

"Fuck the horse ya came here on," Mini said back.

"Bitch, I'll slap the taste outcha mouth," A-K said moving towards her.

Power-Up stepped in before shit got outta hand. "Chill out, A-K," Power-Up said.

"Tell that hoe to chill out, then" A-K stated angrily.

For some reason, A-K and Mini stayed at each other throats. No one ever asked why, but they were all sure that it would come out one day. It seemed like they had one of those love-hate relationships between the two of them.

Jam came out the back office with Keba walking behind him. When Power-Up saw her, he was for sure his heart had skipped a few beats.

"Hey, fellas," Keba said as she walked around to give everyone a hug. Power-Up knew he might've been trippin, but his hug felt like a caressing hug than a normal hug.

Everyone started talking shit for a while about anything and everything you could think of talking about with women in a Beauty Salon. One thing about women in a Beauty Salon is that a nigga can't win shit talkin in there any more than a woman can win talkin shit in a barber shop.

After thirty minutes of bull-shittin, Jam, Power-Up, YoungOne, and A-K busted out.

Dropping everybody off, Jam rode around thinking about giving the game up before it was too late. Deep in his heart, he wanted to be a family man to his two kids and wife. He loved them all more than life itself. He thought to himself: this next pick up I'ma take Power-Up to meet the connect and let him take over. He's ready. Jam knew that he would always have Power-Up's back, but he was tired of living the party life.

Yeah, Jam thought out loud. That's what I'ma do.

YoungOne liked to hit the school zones every day. Even though he was 18 years old that still didn't stop him from checking out the high school girls. Most of them were girls he went to school with before he dropped out. So driving down Winbourne Ave, passing by Istrouma High in his apple red Dodge Magnum on 24's with the six TV's and six-twelves bangin always put all eyes on him; and, he liked it that way. He was well-known around the school, and pretty much knew everyone who attended the school, so when he made a left turn on 38th Street and spotted a lil chick that looked like she was too old to be in high school, he had to know who she was. Because she was carrying what looked to be like school books, he knew she was young. He just hoped not too young.

Beep! Beep! Beep! YoungOne blew his horn to alert the girl, and then pulled up on side of her. "Excuse me? Can I give you a ride?" He knew she would probably say "no," but that's all he could think of to say.

"Hell no! I don't know you," she snapped back.

Beep! Beep! Beep!

"You have cars behind you," the girl said.

"And?" YoungOne said as he continued to ride slowly alongside her. She continued to walk, not even thinking to stop and at least take a peek inside YoungOne's car. This behavior intrigued him and made him want to know bout this chick. "You more important than them," he said smoothly.

She started smiling. YoungOne knew then that he had her. He pulled off then turned on a side street. He grabbed his glock-40, stuck it in the front of his pants, and jumped out the car walking back to meet girl. YoungOne didn't have no game. He was fuckin hoes off his looks and street credibility when he was younger, but now he was fuckin them because of the stuff he got like his money, fresh fits, and cars. He was nervous trying to think of what he was going to say.

"You thought I was leaving huh" YoungOne said upon returning.

"Actually, yes," she said.

"Since you wouldn't accept my offer for a ride, can I walk you home?" YoungOne asked. He was starting to feel his natural confidence arise as he began talking to her.

"Who said I was going home?" she questioned.

"Well, wherever you headed, I'll walk with you," YoungOne said.

"I might be on my way to my man's house," she said with a smirk.

"And he has a beautiful lady like you walking?" YoungOne shot back.

"I might just feel like walking," she stated blushing simultaneously.

"What's your name?" YoungOne asked.

"LaShay."

"It's nice to meet you LaShay. I'm—" She cut him off before he could even finish his introduction.

"I know who you are," she asserted.

Oh, you do? Who am I?" YoungOne asked looking her straight in the eyes.

"They call you 'YoungOne,' right?" She responded.

"Yes, but you can call me Kenny," YoungOne said back.

"Why?" she asked.

"Because you special." YoungOne meant what he said. It was something about this girl that made him feel good. He felt like she wasn't a gold digger, and that she could trust him. That was why he wanted her to call him by his real name.

"What makes me so special?" LaShay said looking at him as if she was entertained.

"Because I said so, YoungOne responded. He couldn't let her know how he really felt at the moment. "How old are you, LaShay?" He was trying to figure some things out about her in his head at the same time of trying to convince her to give him play. But, she still wasn't making it easy for him.

"Old enough," she said as if that should have answered everything about her for him.

"Why you giving me a hard time like I did you something?" he continued. Since I can't have your age, then maybe I can have your number?" YoungOne kept pushing it. He wasn't about to give up on this one.

"I don't give my number out, but I will take yours," she replied.

YoungOne was thinking that if he didn't want this fine and beautiful ass hoe, he would have been tore up. Then again maybe she's not a hoe, he thought, because mostly all the women he holla at, he'd fuck the same night or the next day at the latest. He wrote his number down then reached to put it in her hands. He could feel that her hands were soft like cotton balls, but he quickly let her hand go, leaving his number in her palm. He didn't want to seem too eager. He had to play it cool, so without another word, he smiled at her, and turned back towards the opposite direction. He could feel her looking at him as he walked back to his car.

CHAPTER SEVEN

P ower-Up had been rolling off of two X pills and fuckin
all night long. He was up the next morning starving
and still wide awake. He ate a bowl of cereal, and then decided to go lay in the hot tub for some relaxation.

"Chow call, Power-Up! You gone eat?

"What time is it?"

"6:00 'o clock in the morning."

"Nah, wake me up when you come back."

Power-Up opened his eyes, looked around, and realized
that he was free man, a free man—laying in the hot tub.
He couldn't seem to shake them prison dreams he thought.
That shit type of living really fucks with ya brains. His
phone was sitting nearby on the toilet beeping, letting him
know that he had messages. He rose slowly up out the tub,
grabbed his towel off the rack, and dried off. He wrapped
his towel around his waist, grabbed his phone and walked
into the bedroom. He checked his phone and saw a number he didn't recognize, a few hoes' numbers, a missed call

from Jam, and one from his mama. He hit his moms up first.

"Hey, baby," his mom answered.

"Hey, Ma," Power-Up replied.

"I was waiting for you to come and see me, so I could give you this number but seems like you don't love your mama anymore," she said in a depressing tone.

"C'mon mama, you know that ain't it. I just saw you two days ago anyway. You know I would never stop loving the woman who brought me into this world." Even though he knew she was just joking with him, Power-Up felt like he just had to let her know that. "Now, what number you have for me?"

"Oh, Boo been calling here a lot lately, and I been forgetting to tell you," she said.

It's a good thing his mama couldn't see his face or read his mind at the mention of that name over the phone. It made him think back to all of those years he spent behind bars when a mutha fucka forgets about ya. His mom's voice brought him back into the present moment.

"Keith, did you hear me?" He heard his mom say.

"Yeah, mama, I hear you," Power-Up replied.

"Oh, I thought you hung up the phone," his mom said.

"Nah, I was just wondering what he wanted," Power-Up explained.

"Me too," his mom said. "He never called when you were doing time," his mom concluded.

"What's his number, Ma?"

After she gave him Boo's number, the two of them bull shitted around on the phone for a few minutes. She made him promise that he was coming see her later on then they ended the call with their usual, but never "goodbye" because that meant forever. He would hit Boo up later, he thought, but right now he had to call his nigga Jam back.

Boo was chillin in Prescott, a neighborhood in Baton Rouge, thinking about his next come-up. I don't understand this shit he thought. Fuckin nigga Power-Up came straight outta prison getting money and ain't holla at me since he been home. What that nigga forgot who I am? I raised him in the game. I know that fool not trippin off that jail shit. Fuck him. I told him to come on. I needed to do it big, and that was my come up. One way or another I'ma give that nigga one more day to call me because I know his mama gave him my number. Otherwise, I'm calling back, or I'll go pay her a visit.

Plack! Plack! Boo was startled by the sound of knocking coming from his driver side car door. Boo looked up, relieved that it was his boy bouncy. He rolled down his window and gave Bouncy some pound.

"Damn dawg, you was zoned out. You ain't even seen me walk up on yo car, and you know how we catch these niggaz slippin on a regular. Don't you be gettin caught up," Bouncy warned.

"I was just thinking bout our next move, Bouncy, that's all. This one will have us straight for a while," Boo stated.

"Let's do it," Bouncy said with excitement in his voice. He knew that when Boo had something planned it meant a nice lick.

Jam hit the mute button on A-K's sound system before answering his phone. "What's up, lil brother?" he answered.

"Coolin," was the reply. "Where you at?"

"Riding around with A-K," Jam said.

"Tell him I said 'what it do,'" Power-Up said.

"Nothin but love" he heard A-K's muffled reply.

"Where you niggaz heading?" Power-Up asked.

"Just riding. What you getting into tonight?" Jam asked.

"Man, I'ma pass by Jiggulator tonight," Power-Up said.

"Damn, Power-Up, you stay at the strip clubs," Jam said.

"Dat shit ease ya mind, Dawg," Power-Up replied.

"If you say so," Jam stated, grinning at the same time.

"I'll get back atcha later," Power-Up said.

"Aight," Jam said.

"Aight. One."

CHAPTER EIGHT

It had been two days since YoungOne saw the girl he met walking home from school, and he couldn't seem to stop thinking about her. He'd never felt this way about a female before.She didn't give him her number plus she hadn't called him either.

"Man, I gotta get my head straight," he thought out loud. "I'm trippin and ain't even fucked yet," he said as he checked his phone making sure he didn't see a number he didn't recognize. He wouldn't want to miss this girl's call. Seeing he didn't have any new numbers calling him, he decided to hit his brother up to pass some time.

Ring, Ring! Ring, Ring!

This fool always let his phone ring so you could hear the Boosie & Webbie song play, "Where Them Dollars At."

"What's up Thug?" A-K finally answered.

"Why you be letting the phone ring, and you know that it's me calling?" YoungOne asked feeling irritated.

"You called me, so fuck you," was the reply he got back.

"Fuck you, pussy," YoungOne shot back.

"What's up before I hang up? Calling me up trippin and shit," A-K said.

"Whatcha doing?" YoungOne asked.

"Just dropped Jam off at home." He paused and then continued, "you going to the club tonight?" A-K wanted to know.

"Yeah, but I don't know which one, yet. You going?" YoungOne asked back.

"Yeah, I'm going to Click Side," A-K told him.

"Okay. I'll meet cha there," YoungOne said.

"Aight," A-K replied, "one."

"One," YoungOne said before hanging up the phone.

Bang! Bang! Bang!

"Keith, why are you banging on my door like that?" His mom could always tell whenever Power-Up was the one knocking at the door by the way he banged on it. He'd been hitting the door the same way since he was a little kid.

"Hey, Ma," Power-Up said as she open the door. "Something smells good, like some delicious things being cooked round here." He was instantly hungry just from the smell of his mom's cooking.

"I cooked your favorite. Red beans and rice with fried chicken and corn bread," his mom said.

"Hey, big brotha!" He turned to see his little sister coming towards him.

"How's my lil sis been doing?" Power-Up asked looking at how big she had gotten. It seemed like she was growing right before his eyes.

"I'm good," she replied.

"Keith," his mom began, "you know she has a boyfriend now."

"Mama, you talk too much," his little sister shot back defensively.

"Girl, don't play with me, I'm still yo mama, and I can say whatever I want," his mama explained.

Angela was turning 16 years old and was well developed, so he knew niggaz was coming at her. Power-Up talked to her a lot about men and what they wanted from females, so he felt that Angela was had been well prepared for the games niggaz play.

Power-Up walked into the kitchen and found his two brothers, BabyFace and CryBaby, sitting at the table ready to eat. He gave both of them pound then sat down ready to do the same.

"Man, bout time you came cause we was going to eat without you," BabyFace said.

"Huh bruh," CryBaby always had to add his two cent into shit to be messy.

"Fuck y'all." Power-Up said to both of them.

"Watch your mouth in this house, Keith! You ain't too old to catch an ass whuppin," his mom stated. He couldn't do anything but laugh at his mom thinking that if she did pick up a belt to whip him he'd be hauling ass outta this bitch.

They were all sitting around talking and eating when the house phone started ringing.

"Y'all, eat. Mama going to answer it. That's probably that lil boy for Angela," his mom continued.

"Let me talk to him if that's who calling," BabyFace said.

"Keith, telephone!" Power-Up heard his mom call out to him. He wondered who it could be calling for him because he never gave anybody the number to his mother's house.

Before handing him the phone his mom covered the mouth piece with her hand and whispered in his ear, "This Boo."

Power-Up took the phone, "Hello?"

"Hello, what's up Power-Up?" Boo asked as soon as he heard Power-Up's voice coming through the phone line.

"I'm good, Boo," he replied.

"What? You been dodging me or something?" Boo asked.

"Dodging you for what?" Power-Up decided to let him play himself out to see where this nigga was bout to bring this shit.

"I don't know. You been out almost a year and you never holla?" Boo asked again.

Power-Up was thinking that this nigga had to be trippin or losing his fuckin mind or something.

"Holla atcha for what, Boo?" Power-Up said trying to control his emotions as to what he really wanted to say to this scum fool. But, he played along.

"Damn, lil nigga it's like that now?" Boo continued.

Power-Up was tired of talking and playing games with this nigga, so he told him to spit it out. "Man, whatcha want Boo?" Power-Up questioned.

"I see you don't wanna have a lil conversation so I'ma be straight up," he said. "Man, I'm hurting out here. I need you to put me on. I wanna shine like you lil nigga," he explained.

Power-Up took the phone from his ear and looked at it for a second or two. When he put it back to his ear, he decided to drop it on Boo as to what it was gonna be between the two of them.

"Boo, check this out. I don't have nothing against you for not keeping it gutta with me when I was on lock, but, dawg, I don't fuck with cha like that," Power-Up stated. Now that all of the pretending had been removed, Power-Up felt like he could say whatever was on his mind.

"I guess I gotta take what I want from you," Boo finally had the nerves to spit out.

"I guess you do," Power-Up shot back.

"I gotcha, Power-Up," Boo stated.

"Fuck you, Boo!" Power-Up replied then hung up the phone and went back in the kitchen to start eating his meal. In that moment he realized that in some ways he was more like his brother, CryBaby, than he thought. He always had to have the last word, too.

CHAPTER NINE

After A-K dropped him off at his home, Jam thought he'd hop on his Yamaha 1100 and take it for a spin. As he began to back out of the driveway, his wife, Tanarsha, pulled up in her 500 Benz, stepped out in her nurse's uniform, and all of his plans just disappeared. She looked so damn sexy in that nurse's uniform. Tanarsha stood at 5'4 inches tall and 140 pounds. She was a size B cup in the breasts, light brown eyes to match her smooth Hershey's complexion, and shoulder length hair. All of those qualities had attracted Jam into proposing marriage to her. Plus, she was the most loyal woman he'd ever met in his life.

"Hey there, sexy," Jam said greeting her with a smile. "Looks like you could use a good massage," Jam said, as he gave her a nice warm tongue kiss.

"I'll accept the massage on one condition," she said.

"And what condition may that be, baby?" Jam asked.

"Only if it leads us both to being naked in the bedroom, engaging in hot passionate love making" she said looking into his eyes with those big beautiful brown eyes of hers. Jam liked the sound of that, so he picked his wife up off her feet and carried her in the house. He hit the code to the alarm system and forgot all about her full-body massage because he was too busy giving her firm ass a nice one while he whispered in her ear to meet him in the shower in two minutes. His wife took off to the master bedroom to get undressed.

After enjoying time with the main family Power-Up took a ride to check on a few of his spots across the river in Plaquemine Parish to kill three birds with one stone: One, killing time before he went to make it rain in the Strip Club, Two. Check on his money, and Three. Think about what this nigga Boo said. He lit up his purple blunt, grabbed his car stereo remote, turned his volume up to number six, and let the 'Big Head' mix cd play.

Boo called his dawg Bouncy up to see if he was ready for the game plan because what he had in mind was bigger than the lil petty robberies they were doing.

"Say, Bouncy," Boo said over the phone, "are you ready to get money?"

"Fuckin right," Bouncy responded back. He always was a nigga who had a hustle game dealing drugs, but he just couldn't seem to make it to the next levels of the game. The highest he'd ever reached was to a four and a half selling rock, which was better than nothing. Boo started running down his game plan down.

"Bouncy, I wanna start a hitting licks clique," Boo said.

"Man, we already do dat now," Bouncy said as if he didn't have any idea what the fuck Boo was talking about.

"Man, I'm talking more niggaz," Boo said starting to get agitated with Bouncy for being so fuckin dumb.

"What 'u mean?" Bouncy asked still not seeing the point Boo was trying to make.

"Bouncy, you remember Seven from Glen Oaks who use to rob with us?" Boo asked.

"Yeah! Nigga, how can I forget that fool? All he wanna do is put that iron on a mutha fucka every lick we hit. That's why we had to back up off that nigga from making us hot," Bouncy explained.

"I wanna include him and one more into our plan. We gonna be called the "Hittin Lick Clique." As soon as Boo finished that statement, another thought came to him on who the fourth nigga in their clique could be. His cousin Buck. Buck always had a habit of bucking up ready to get into some shit. That's how he earned the name Buck.

Boo continued on telling Bouncy how he needed niggaz who was ready, could be trusted, and those who he chose, it had to be them or nobody at all.

The Club was packed when A-K pulled up. The line was looking like it wasn't' moving. Fortunately, all that didn't matter to A-K because he never waited in line. All he had to do was to give the doorman a one-hundred dollar bill and keep it VIP-style. A-K jumped out his whip, put his Glock-40 on his side, and headed to the front of the line when a set of eyes caught his attention. The girl was standing there in a pair True Religion jeans and a True Religion off-the-shoulder top with some 6 inch pumps. Damn! He thought. She sure did know how to wear that outfit! He had to stop and see why this bad bitch was standing in line when clearly she was supposed to be doing it VIP-style with him. He just grabbed her hand and pulled her with him. At the same time she turned around, grabbed her friend's hand and was pulling this other woman with her. A-K looked at her side-ways, and she must have read his mind because before he could say anything, she spoke.

"This my friend, and we came here together," she said. Her friend was also nice-looking and dressed in the same outfit but just a different color.

"Let's roll," A-K said. They reached the front of the line and he recognized the door man off top.

"What's up, No Neck?" A-K greeted him.

"My man, A-K, whatcha have tonight," No-Neack responded.

"The usual," A-K said, which meant that he was strapped, "and these two sexy ladies."

"You know what it do," No-Neck said. A-K handed him $400 then walked in the club and headed straight to the VIP section to wait on his dawg YoungOne.

Back outside, waiting in line was Boo, feeling some type of way about the situation that just went down with A-K. Look at this lil nigga, he thought. Who the fuck he think he is taking them two bitches I had my eyes on in the club with him—and he go straight to the front of the line like he own this shit. But, Boo knew how the game went. He knew that when you doing it big like A-K was, you could make moves like that. Soon, he thought, I'll be doing it like dat, too. Boo wanted to turn around and leave out the line from feeling played by how A-K pulled dat stunt in front of everybody. Fuck dat, he thought. I won't let this nigga stop me from having fun tonight. I need to check this clown out anyway.

"Oooohh, Jam, baby!! Yes!! Right there!!! Aaaahhhh!" Jam was sucking on his wife clit like it was a blow pop with the bubble gum in the middle, and he was trying to reach the center of it. Jam rose up off his knees then Tanarsha grabbed his dick and propped her left leg up on the edge of the tub and placed the head of his swollen penis on her throbbing pussy. She rubbed it up and down because she knew dat drove him crazy.

Jam couldn't take it no more so he grabbed his dick out her hand and inserted himself in the softest place on earth. They both found the rhythm they wanted and climaxed like it was their first time. They breathed in and out heavily until their bodies calmed back down. Jam washed up and jumped out the shower to let his wife take care her hygiene like women do.

That's it, he thought. He had made his mind up. As he stood in the bedroom, he knew in that moment, that it was time. He was leaving the game alone. He had enough money, his wife was the head nurse at the General Hospital, and his two kids had trust funds for when they grew up. He had no more need for the game. He was getting to old for the shit. He was ready for the simple life. He was brought back to reality out his deep thoughts at the sound of his wife's voice calling his name.

"Jam," he heard her call.

"Yeah baby?" he responded.

"Don't be sleep when I come out. I'm ready for round two," she said.

"That's what's up, baby," Jam said, but as soon as his head hit the pillow it was all over. Sleep had overwhelmed his old ass.

Power-Up pulled in the parking lot of the strip club and instantly his dick started to rise knowing that pussy would be flocking all around the place. After riding around taking care of business, he drove home, took a quick shower, then threw on his Lacoste outfit and a pair of Jordan G-Nikes. He decided his platinum 'I'm Free' chain and bracelet would be the perfect jewel pieces to set the outfit off. He counted out six thousand dollars then got excited at the thought of making it rain in the club with all eyes on him. He grabbed his lil money sack and slid out his car.

As soon as Power-Up hit the door of the club, all eyes were on him. Or at least that's what he was thinking. Paranoid, he thought maybe it was just the purple or the half of an x-pill he was rollin off of that had him trippin like dat. He made his way to the bar and ordered himself some Hennessy with coke. He downed it, then brought two bottles of water and walked towards the stage.

"Hey baby, I thought you wasn't gonna show up tonight," said one of the strippers named Juicy. Power-Up had been fuckin her since he started coming to the club, and even though she was built like a brick house, he wanted some new ass tonight. One thing he liked about Juicy is that she knew that he just wanted to fuck with no strings attached.

"Baby, you know it's been about two weeks since you been here, so we have two new dancers from Atlanta that I think you might like. They come out next," Juicy said.

"They badder than you?" Power-Up asked her.

"I'ma bad bitch, Power-Up, but these two bitches give me a run for my money," she said.

"They selling dat pussy?"" Power-Up asked her.

"I don't know but a nigga of yo caliber could make it happen. Now watch me walk," Juicy said then walked off smiling. Juicy used to always tell him she never tricked. She danced to take care of herself and her nephew she'd been raising since her sister was killed. But, enough money and the right words had him all up in that juicy ass and he did mean *ass*.

Boo had finally made it inside the club. He was coming through to act a fool but seeing A-K threw a monkey wrench in his plans, now he would just have to watch him to see how the dude rolled. Boo looked around and did not see A-K, so he made his way near the VIP section. Even though he couldn't be in there, he figured it would be a good idea to at least be close by.

YoungOne walked through the club after getting off the phone with A-K telling him to come up to the VIP section. As soon as YoungOne passed by, Boo noticed him. That's dat other lil nigga right there, Boo thought as he spotted YoungOne. I should catch 'em tonight and put that iron in both they faces to send a message. But, that will only put those clowns on alert, and I want big things, not pocket change. Tonight is the start of the life I'm bout to be living, Boo thought. Watch and observe is the happenings.

The lights on the stage dimmed for nearly twenty seconds, and all you could see was a green glow in the dark thong set and another one, which was yellow. Then, Nelly's song 'Tip Drill' started blaring through the speakers, and the lights on the stage came back on. Whoa! Power-Up could see what Juicy was saying about the two Atlantian strippers. They were coco brown skinned, long Toni Braxton hair do's, beautiful, and built ford tough with green eyes dat looked real wicked.

Before Power-Up knew it, he himself, was throwing bundles of money at the stage for these two hoes. That lil six grand he brought with him was gone in a flash. He had to get one of them and he knew that Juicy would be the one to make it happen. They didn't call him Power-Up for nothing. It didn't take him long before he spotted Juicy, and told her to tell the new dancers to come see him for a lap dance.

"Waaah, what's up, A-K?" YoungOne hollered.

"Coolin. Chillin with these two Lafayette ladies. This my brother, YoungOne, I was telling y'all bout. This Brandy, who has been waiting on you, and her friend NayNay. They came to have a good night of fun in fuckin," A-K said with excitement in his voice.

"SShiiit!! I'm in the right place," YoungOne said as he sat down and joined the group.

Power-Up was waiting on the twins to come and give him a lap dance. In the meantime, he came up with a plan. Quickly, he counted out a thousand dollars from the money he had left in his pocket. He made a phone call to his dude Moe who had been on lock with him but had since been home a few months. He told him what he was about to do. The twins walked in the room and he started playing it cool, acting like he was in deep conversation on the phone. He continued his conversation for about two minutes and then told Moe to hold on. He turned towards the twins and told them that he apologized but something came up and he had to go. They look on their faces said: "I know this nigga didn't waste our time." Power-Up pulled out the knot of money, wrote his number on one of the hundred dollar bills, handed it to them and told them to call him tomorrow. He took a sip of his drink, stood up, and walked out of the club.

CHAPTER TEN

"Where the fuckin money at nigga? You playin with my emotions with this lying shit! You know what, YoungOne, bring the kids in here." Jam was confused hearing this nigga with a gun to his head tell his boy to bring his kids to the room they were in. YoungOne walked in holding Jam's two year old son and his five year old daughter's hand. The nigga pointed his gun at the daughter and before Jam could say anything, Boom! The gun went off.

Kiss, Kiss, Kiss, Kiss.

Jam awoke from his dream and became aware that someone was kissing him. Then, his wife voice drifted into his brains. "I told you don't go to sleep I wanted seconds. And why are you looking like you seen a ghost?" His wife asked as she lay beside him in bed. "Baby, I just had the scariest dream of my life," Jam explained to his wife. He went on to tell his wife about YoungOne selling him out but he was sure to leave out the part about their daughter getting shot in the stomach at close range.

A-K liked to get his stunt on, especially around people who didn't know him. Feeling good off the x-pills and Codeine had him in the zone. "Man, fuck, I feel like buying the whole damn club drinks," he said out loud.

"Every time you get to rolling hard you get all friendly and shit," YoungOne said. But he also knew that was how those pills would have him too, so he couldn't judge too much. A-K grabbed the bottle of Remy Ma, jumped up and walked to the bar.

"Bartender!" He shouted out to get attention. "What's up, A-K?" the bartender answered.

"What is he doing?" NayNay asked YoungOne.

"Ain't no telling," YoungOne replied. "It looks like he buying everybody drinks like he wanted to do."

"Oooh! Look how that girl all up on him," Brandy said looking over at her friend.

NayNay jumped up thinking, *"not for long"* and headed toward the bar.

A-K handed the bartender two thousand dollars and said, "Make some drinks for everybody in this bitch."

"Excuse me. He belongs to me tonight," NayNay said to the girl with an evil look in her eyes. The Girl looked up at A-K and all he did was shrug his shoulders then walked off with NayNay back toward the DJ booth.

YoungOne was talking with Brandy about the strawberry festival event that Lafayette holds every year when he recognized the same eyes on him from the moment he walked to the VIP section. "I know I ain't trippin but that fuckin nigga watching me" YoungOne said out loud not realizing how loud his voice was.

"Who watching you?" Brandy asked.

"Nobody," YoungOne responded.

"Well, I'm watching you at the same time wondering how big yo dick is," Brandy said looking into his face with pure lust in her eyes.

Inside the DJ booth A-K handed the DJ some money and grabbed the mike. "Listen up! Everybody! For the ones who don't know me I'm A-K and that's my lil brother YoungOne up there in the VIP section. We having a good time, so we want you all to do the same on the love. Drinks of your choice at the bar." The club went into shouts and whistles. Being satisfied A-K headed back to the VIP section feeling himself.

"I think that I need to move around because this the second time me and this lil nigga done caught eye contact. His boy, his brother, A-K, or whoever the fuck he think he is, just bought the whole club drinks. I might be hating, but I too do need a few drinks for free. Soon, it will be me, Boo, who will be stunting hard like that. After downing a few drinks Boo left tipsy and feeling played on how them young ass niggaz took the hoe he wanted upstairs to the VIP section then brought drinks for the club. These fools think they can't be touched or something. I'm the fuckin dawg.

A-K was squeezing NayNay ass on their way back to the VIP section thinking how he would put that pound game down tonight. When they entered YoungOne was laid back while girl was sucking his dick. NayNay looked at A-K and said it was time to "roll out beacuse her pussy was drippin wet.

"YoungOne, we headed to the Hilton. I'ma get the double rooms," A-K said. He knew when they do the double-room-thang they switching bitches. So A-K had to make sure

YoungOne knew what was going down. "Man, you heard me?"

"I fuckin heard you, don't you see I'm getting my pipe cleaned," YoungOne said in response. He was trying to pay attention to what A-K was saying and at the same time concentrate on what was going on with his dick. "Which one we going to---on College Drive? I'ma meet cha there," he concluded and went back to getting his dick hit up.

A-K was thinking that ole girl must be retarded with her head game because the nasty bitch never stopped. He must check her head game out. He wanted to get him some head on the way to the room but the girl was following him in her car. He tried to get her to leave her shit but her reaction said it all.

"Nigga, this Baton Rouge, where niggaz ratchet as a mutha fucka. I ain't leaving my shit here," she said. She was right on that, and he couldn't argue the point. Leaving a fresh painted Lexus on 20's in a club parking lot after closing hours meant that it would certainly disappear in minutes or be stripped on site.

"Who this pussy for?" Jam asked in a heat of passion to his wife.

"You daddy," his wife responded in short breaths of moans.

"What's my name?" He continue to entice his wife with words of passion because that shit turned her on.

"Ooooh! Ooooh! Aaaahhh! Stop baabby! Uhuuhhh, right there!" Jam was licking his wife's Tanarsha pussy but his mind was still on that crazy dream and trying to get some kind of understanding out it.

"Wanna see how you taste, baby?" he asked his wife then heard her say, "uh huh." Jam laid on top his wife then stuck his tongue in her mouth.

"I taste good. I see why you love tasting me. Ha, ha, ha. Roll over now. My turn to taste that big dick of yours," Tanarsha said in a sexy like voice.

"No. Climb on top and ride it like a cow girl," Jam said. And she did. The way Tanarsha pussy felt, you wouldn't think she spit two kids out. Her pussy was still tight like a virgin. Easing down on Jam's manhood taking slow strides until her pussy walls was satisfied, Tanarsha started what she learnt from reading one of Zane books, 'Ride 'em Hard' and that's what she did.

"Who this dick for?" She demanded Jam answer.

"Uuuuhhh, you baby! Aaaahhh. I love youuuu babbbby," Jam said in complete satisfaction. Tanarsha spent around and put her feet flat on the bed with her hands on Jam's chest and started going in circular motions then up and down.

"I'M COMMMING! AAAAHHHH!!! COME WITH ME BABY! Damn this pussy good!!" Jam expressed to his wife. Tanarsha was also on the verge of nutting. Just by the way Jam was talking to her had her ready to explode. Soon as he came, she did too then they both just laid there in silence listening to each other hearts beat.

A-K texted YoungOne to let him know room 225 was where it was all going down. He lay across the bed sippin codeine and smokin some fire ass purple while flipping through TV stations looking for a nice flick to watch until girl freshened up. Bitch didn't have to do all that. He was thinking, ready to get his freak on as NayNay walked out the bathroom wearing red lingere. He just laid there. He was stuck, too loaded to move. He was higher than the twin towers and still smokin.

Knock, Knock, Knock.

"Somebody knocking?" NayNay asked as she stood there in her lingerie. A-K was so zoned out of his fuckin mind that all he could manage to say was, "yep."

"That's probably Brandy 'nem," she said.

"Who dat?" A-K asked as he approached the door. When he heard the reply he knew for sure who it was.

"Who the fuck you think, nigga," YoungOne said through the door. A-K opened the door then walked back to the bed before he fell out because he could've sworn the room was spinning.

"I'm going take a quick shower," Brandy said when she walked in.

"Y'all bout whatever?" A-K asked then looked from one girl to the other.

"What you mean?" NayNay asked back.

"Switching partners," YoungOne spoke up seeing NayNay looking damn delicious.

"We're down," Brandy said, "I'll be right back." She went to the bathroom and before she made it back NayNay was sucking YoungOne dick while A-K was eating her pussy from the back. Brandy was kinda mad they started without her. She immediately started sucking A-K dick to join in.

Twenty-five minutes later YoungOne stood up, pulled NayNay from between A-K's legs then moved her to the bed and started eating her pussy. The rest of the night went on with fuckin, suckin, sixty-nine, a whole fuck fest until none of 'em could move.

Man I wanted to knock them fucking twins' pussy out the frame, Power-Up was thinking to himself, but he knew he had to play it that way because he wanted both of them. He drove home and laid' back in his Jacuzzi and fell off into a deep sleep.

Keba was driving around in her Lexus with no particular destination in mind. She did it sometimes to clear her mind when somethings needed to be cleared out in her head. She stopped at the red light with a few cars in front of her and was about to reach for her lip gloss when she noticed a picture on her dash board. She picked it up and saw it was the picture she took of her brother, Jam, Power-Up, A-K, and YoungOne. Keba stared at the picture as if she missed seeing something from the last umpteen times she had stared and looked at it. No one really knew but the truth of the matter was she only kept the picture with her everywhere she went because Power-Up was in it. She didn't want anyone to be alerted of her feelings for Power-Up. Having a picture with all four of them wouldn't seem too obvious to anyone if they happened to glance up at the picture on her dashboard.

"Besides, I'm tired of this nigga I'm with, and I don't know why," she began to speak out loud. "He treats me damn good. I'm financially secure, and he still breaks bread. Plus, the sex is good. What could it be that's got me thinking something ain't straight? I really think I know what's wrong with me. I been feeling this way ever since Power-Up been home. I have never been the type of woman who would deny herself what she wanted in life and I ain't gonna start now. I must have him even if Jam won't approve of it. Forget Jam, he's my damn brother and not my daddy. Not even my daddy could stop the way I feel when I think about or see that nigga." The light turned green and she drove off.

Jam was lying back thinking, when his thoughts went on his lil sister. Keba was a good girl who never had to go through the things a lot of young women go through growing up because her big brother always kept her straight. All he wanted in return was for her to finish school, go to college, and get a degree in Business Management so he could turn dirty money into clean money. After doing that, Keba took up the trade of a Beautician and for the most part had been successful. He was so proud of her.

Chirp, Chirp, Chirp.

Where the fuck these niggaz at? I been calling their phones all morning, Jam thought. He was about to hang up the phone when Power-Up picked up.

"What's up, nigga," Power-Up said sounding sleepy.

"Man, I was about to hang up. You sleep?" Jam asked.

"Dawg, I fell asleep in the Jacuzzi last night and still in this bitch. The water is cold as a mutha fucka," Power-Up replied sitting up straight in the Jacuzzi.

"You was with YoungOne and A-K because they not answering their cell phones neither," Jam explained.

"Nah, I talked to them yesterday sometime," Power-Up said.

"When you get together, come to the Sports Bar, try to call them lil niggaz, and let 'em know to meet us up there," Jam said.

"Fa sho, One," Power-Up said and was about to click off when Jam continued.

"Oh, and Power-Up, don't take all day," Jam stressed.

"I'm not. It's nine-thirty so I'll be there by a quarter to eleven," Power-Up said.

"One," Jam said.

"One," Power-Up responded then clicked off.

YoungOne woke up hearing A-K's phone rappin that Lil Boosie, and his phone vibrating on the lamp stand next to the bed. "A-K, yo phone ringing, nigga," he said.

"Answer it," A-K said grouchily.

"My shit going off too," YoungOne said. Not noticing the number, he was hesitant to answer but he did anyway.

"Yeah," he answered.

"That's how you greet people in the morning?" The voice on the other end said.

"People shouldn't call this early," YoungOne shot back.

"Well, I guess I've picked the wrong time to call you," the voice said.

"Maybe you did. Now, who is this?" YoungOne asked.

"Ha, ha, ha, ha! Now you interested," the caller said.

"Not really. I was gonna tell you I'll get back atcha later, but since you said it like dat, yeah, I'm interested in who this is?" YoungOne questioned.

"This LaShay," the caller said, finally.

A-K finally picked up his phone and saw that it was his dude calling him. "What's up?" he asked when he answered.

"I been calling you and YoungOne all morning. Is he with you?" Jam asked.

"Yeah, we at the room with two freaks from Lafayette," A-K said.

"I'm over at the Sport Bar, and Power-Up's on the way over here. Y'all try and be here in an hour," Jam said.

"Aight," A-K said trying to get off the phone. Not dat he didn't wanna holla at Jam, he was just stupid tired as a mutha fucka. "We'll be there," A-K said.

"One," Jam said.

"One," A-K replied.

YoungOne jumped up and went to the bathroom so he could talk privately. "Hey, baby, I thought you'd never call and was bout to come looking for you," YoungOne said with excitement in his voice.

"Yeah, right," LaShay said, smiling from ear to ear.

"Girl, I'm serious."

Bam, Bam, Bam!

"Man, don't you see me in here?" YoungOne hollered.

"Fuck that! You on the phone not using the toilet, and I gotta piss," A-K responded urgently.

"You shoulda used the other one," YoungOne said angrily.

"Fuck all dat. I can't wait. Plus, Jam wants us to meet him at the Sports Bar in an hour," A-K explained.

"Aight, now get the fuck out," YoungOne responded. A-K walked out and slammed the door behind him.

"Hello?" LaShay said in a confused manner.

"Yeah, I'm still here. My bad, that's my crazy ass brother A-K," YoungOne explained.

"It's cool," LaShay said laughing at them.

"Why you laughing?" YoungOne asked jokingly.

"Y'all crazy, boy," she responded.

"This your cell phone number?" he asked her.

"Yes," she said without hesitation.

"I need to call you later if that's okay," YoungOne told her.

"Alright, do that," she said.

"I sure will," YoungOne replied letting her know he was serious.

Boo contacted Buck and Seven then had them meet him and Bouncy on Prescott. Once they arrived, he explained what the plan was gonna be. Every one of 'em had a job to do to start off the mission that had to be accomplished. But really it was all in Boo's plan to do it that way. Bouncy was to start going to get his hair cut at the barber shop on Myrtle Street located in the South which belonged to Power-Up. Buck's job was to start getting his car washed at the detail shop that Jam owned which was setup in Scotlandville where niggaz be moving heavyweight shit.

Seven's job was the hardest, which was to scope out the gambling shack in Port Allen because now they had to all produce money for the four days he was using to get in cause you couldn't start with less than two thousand dollars.

Boo's job was the easiest being he was dealing with women who do hair because he had dreadlocks. Keba's Beauty Salon would be like taking candy from a baby, but Boo also had to watch Jam's crib because he was the one he wanted to catch slippin with his kids and make him be the real come up.

CHAPTER ELEVEN

I f Jam wouldn't have called Power-Up he'd probably still be out. He must have been as tired as a prostitute who'd been on her feet all night. Power-Up threw on his dark blue Coogi shirt and pants, his Coogi socks with the matching dark blue Coogi shoes then placed on his platinum 'Gutta Boyz' chain and left out headed to the Sports Bar.

YoungOne wanted to lie back between legs of either one of the freaks, but knowing if he did, they wouldn't make it to the Sports Bar, so he woke the hoes up and told them that him and A-K had to go. He told them he would pay for the rooms so they could get some sleep before driving back to Lafeyette. Brandy thanked him and A-K then gave both of them a kiss on the neck and woke up NayNay, so she could say her goodbyes to two niggaz who brought them to a night of ecstasy. They all exchanged numbers and promised each other to hook up again.

"Before y'all leave," NayNay said, "can I at least suck a dick to send y'all off?"

"I wish it could be so, but time is not on our side," A-K said.

"Well, I want y'all to know them 'Gutta Boyz' chains is off the hook. Maybe we can join forces and we'll be called "'Gutta Girlz,'" NayNay said and licked her tongue trying to seduce them.

"We're outta here before our minds be changed," YoungOne said grabbing A-K by the arm then backed out the door.

Jam was shooting pool by himself when Power-Up came bouncing through the door looking like a boss. Jam not the type to be too flashy. But, seeing the 'Gutta Boyz' chain Power-Up had on made him wish he wore his platinum 'Gutta Boyz' chain that Power-Up bought him, A-K, and YoungOne. One night while they all was in New Orleans at the Essence festivals, Power-Up, rolling on three pills feeling emotional, telling all of them how much he loved them, and that since he considered them his brothers from different mothers that they had to all be known as the 'Gutta Boyz.' From that day until now, that's what it been.

"Whats up, nigga?" Power-Up asked as he walked up to the pool table.

"The same thang. I was just thinking when I saw that chain on your neck how hard we was going that night," Jam reminded him.

"Huh bra, we was out our fuckin minds that night. You got in touch with them lil niggaz?" Power-Up asked.

"Yeah. They was at the room with some hoes from Lafeyette," Jam said.

"Speaking of hoes, dawg the Strip Club I be hitting got two new strippers who are twins, and, Jam, them bitches something serious," Power-Up told him.

"How much you tricked off? Ha, ha ha!" Jam said laughing.

"Close to ten grand," Power-Up admitted.

"Man, you crazy. But, like they say, it ain't trickin if you got it. You slept with both of 'em?" Jam asked.

"I didn't fuck none of them but, believe me, I will. I may be able to use them somehow," Power-Up concluded.

"I'll give you that, Power-Up, you always thinking on situations. Rack the balls, I ain't beat yo ass in a minute," Jam said.

"You know you can't fuck with me fool. Remember how I used to bust dat ass up in the bing?" Power-Up said reminding Jam how he had him mad at everybody because he used to hold the pool table down.

"Oh, that's old shit dude. I wasn't on top of my game then. Me and YoungOne be putting that pop on you and A-K," Jam said.

"Let's see how you do by yourself," Power-Up shot back.

"I'm confident," Jam said.

"Me, too," Power-Up retaliated.

"Make a bet," Jam said.

"Make it light on yo 'self," Power-Up inserted.

"How you wanna do it?" Jam asked.

"I said make it light on yo'self," Power-Up reiterated.

"Best out of three," Jam said.

"Aight. What's the bet?" Power-Up asked. Jam started smiling.

"What?" Power-Up said not caring what it was because he knew Jam would lose anyway.

"I win, no strip clubs for a month," Jam said.

"Bet. I win, you go with me for two months," Power-Up shot back.

"Bet that," Jam said. "Flip a coin to see who break."

"You can break. I'ma beat cha anyway, Jam," Power-Up said as he grabbed the rack to set up the balls.

A-K was calling YoungOne to see if he had left his house yet. He'd never seen the white four-door Delta-88 pull up on the side of him at the corner of Chippewa and Plank Road. Before he realized what was going, an assault rifle was pointed out the passenger window.

"Hello, Hello, Heelllooo!"

"What the fuck, A-K!"

YoungOne at first thought A-K was calling playing games with him until he kept hearing the gun shots in the background. In his panic state of mind he quickly dialed Jam number.

It was one game apiece. Power-Up had two high balls left while Jam was about to shoot the eight ball in the right corner pocket when his phone started vibrating on his side. Jam looked at the number then grabbed the phone. "What's up, Thug?" he answered.

"Man, A-K just called me up, and when I answered the phone all I heard was gun shots. I thought he was calling playing games until I heard tires screeching then I knew it wasn't a game," YoungOne explained still sounding fucked up behind the shit.

"You tried calling back?" Jam asked then dropped the pool stick walking towards the door telling Power-Up they was leaving. "Where you at right now?" Jam asked YoungOne.

Power-Up looked at his phone to make sure it was on because whoever Jam was on the phone with wasn't giving him no good news. The expression on Jam's face said it all.

"YoungOne, get in ya car and ride around to see if you spot his car." Power-Up knew then it had something to do with A-K.

"Call his number back and then call me back in five minutes. Me and Power-Up gonna split up and try to see if we can spot his car," Jam said then clicked off.

"What happened?" Power-Up asked. Jam explained what YoungOne said happened when A-K called him. Power-Up gave Jam pound then walked outside to his car with Jam following. "I'ma call you every five minutes," he explained to Jam. "I'ma drive through Ghosttown and come out through Brookstown heading toward A-K's house," Power-Up concluded.

"One," Jam said.

"One," Power-Up replied.

"Oh," Jam said, "by the way, I won the bet." Then he got in his car to go on the search for A-K.

What the fuck?! Bitch ass nigga tried to take me out the game. A-K was thinking to himself as he was walking down Calumet Street after ramming his ride into somebody's house trying to dodge the bullets that was ripping through it. Shit! I forgot my damn phone! It's cool though, long as I got my forty-five. Whoever dat was will pay for missing them shots. I'll never forget that car long as I live. A-K walked to the Yang Store, called the police to report his car stolen then called YoungOne to come get him.

YoungOne was riding around trying to keep his mind focus thinking the worst but praying for the best when his phone started ringing.

"Hello?"

"Man, you won't believe what just went down," A-K started to explain. But, YoungOne didn't have time for all that right now. He was feeling at ease from hearing his dude's voice. YoungOne cut him off asking, "where you at?"

"I'm at the Yang Store on Plank Road down the street from Domino's. Come get me ASAP. I'ma be inside the store," A-K said.

"I'll be there in bout seven minutes cause I'm coming through C. C. Lockdown right now," YoungOne explained.

"Aight, one," A-K said.

"One," YoungOne replied.

Jam knew for sure he told YoungOne to call him every five minutes. And now the lil nigga was not even answering his damn phone. Well, he thought, let me hit Power-Up to see if YoungOne called him.

"What's up?" Power-Up answered hoping to hear that Jam found A-K.

"YoungOne called you?" Jam asked.

"Nah," Power-Up replied.

"I told that nigga to hold on," Jam said looking at his phone to see who was calling. "Dat's YoungOne calling, don't hang up, Power-Up."

"Aight," Power-Up said.

Soon as Jam clicked the phone over before he could say something YoungOne started running it.

"A-K just called me and he's at the Yang Store on Plank Road. I'm on my way to pick him up now," YoungOne explained.

"Cool, meet me at Keba's since y'all close by and call me when you pick him up," Jam said.

"Aight," YoungOne said then hung up.

Jam clicked back over and told Power-Up A-K's straight and to meet them at Keba's.

Thinking about going to Keba's Beauty Salon brought excitement to Power-Up because that gave him a chance to see his baby Keba. He knew she was gonna greet him with a sensational hug and kiss on the cheek, which always sent chills down his spine. His phone ringing brought him out the zone he was in. He hated when a mutha fucka called him private. Whoever this is better be happy I'm feeling straight dat my dude A-K good on some shit or they would get the voice mail.

"Hello?"

"Hello, Mr. Stunna, Man," the voice said on the other end of the phone.

"You must have the wrong number because last I re-membered my name was Power-Up," he said to the voice.

"I learned that from yo friend, but the way you gave seven thousand dollars away would make anybody call you Mr. Stunna Man," the voice said.

"Oh!" Then it hit Power-Up who the voice belonged to. "Okay, this the twins from Jiggulators right?"

"I see you don't forget who you give yo money to," the twin said.

"Nah, it's not that. I just don't forget something I like or want," Power-Up shot back at her.

"That's so sweet," she said.

"I'm talking to one of y'all or two?" Power-Up asked. "Just one, but we come as a package deal," she said.

"Now dat so sweet," PowerUp said with all smiles.

"We don't come easy though. You must earn the package deal," she then said.

"How can I do dat?" Power-Up responded and feeling like he could do anything to receive what he wanted out here in these streets.

"Well, Mr. Stunna Man," she was saying but Power-Up cut her off.

"That's not my name," he said.

"You don't like dat name, I see," she said in a cool like voice.

"No, I don't. Call me 'Power-Up'. You got that?"

Her silence on the other end let Power-Up know she got his point.

"Now I was about to say you started off good to earn the package deal," she said in that cool-like sexy voice.

"I tend to succeed at things I wanna accomplish," Power-Up was telling her when realized he had pulled up in front of Keba's.

"I like a man with a lot of confident but it's a shame when they can't back it up," she said.

"Ha, ha, ha, ha!" All Power-Up could do was laugh at the girl.

"What's so funny?" She decided to ask.

"Just trippin off yo last statement. But look, let me earn some points," Power-Up said to get to the point of her calling him anyway.

"How's that?" She asked but knowing where he was taking this.

"Let me take y'all out to eat and show y'all a good time," Power-Up told her.

"It's ya lucky night because we off tonight," she explained.

"I tend to be a lucky man sometimes," Power-Up said.

"What time can we be expecting ya?" she asked.

"Seven-thirty," Power-Up responded.

"We'll be waiting," she said.

"What's y'all names?" Power-Up asked her.

"The same as our stage names," she replied.

"I never knew y'all stage names," Power-Up responded back.

"You lost earning points for that. But, it's Meka and Mecko," she said.

"How's I'm suppose to get in touch? I don't even know y'all number or address," Power-Up said.

"I'll call you at seven-thirty. That's the time you said huh?" She said in that cool-like voice of hers.

"That's right," Power-Up responded. "By the way, which one of you I'm talking to?" Power-Up asked her.

"Meka," she responded then hung up.

He got out his car and headed toward Keba's. As he was walking up, A-K, YoungOne, and Jam was standing in front of Keba's Salon looking at him stupidly as he approached them. He gave all of them pound then asked A-K what was going on.

A-K began telling Power-Up about the white Delta-88 pulling up on side him and that the people in it started shooting. He said he knew that if he woulda been a second later looking up, his life would be over.

"Who you pissed off?" Power-Up asked.

"Nobody, thug. I've been chillin since dat last shit happened with them clowns in Dixie," A-K responded.

"That's who it probably was then," YoungOne said.

"All of us put word out that we offering two grand for whoever finds out ```who that car belongs to," Jam said then walked in the beauty salon. A-K, YoungOne, and Power-Up followed pursuit and walked in the salon, too.

Inside of Keba's, women was doing what they do very often in a beauty salon, sitting around shoo-shooin about men.

"Girl, I know dat's right," Yoshi said slapping hands with Kimmie for saying a nigga gotta be working a nine inch or better and know how to use his tool to satisfy her.

"Long as his tongue game sick with it, he don't have to have a big dick," one of the girls said. She was getting her hair in kosha braids.

"Nigga better have some money to get some of these goodies," Shaunda said looking at the Gutta Boyz walking in.

Keba walked from around the chair by one of the women's hair she was washing and gave Jam and his boyz hugs. After greeting all of 'em Keba and Jam walked off to her office like always to discuss business.

"A-K you ain't been shootin 'em up bang, bang lately, huh?" Mini said but wasn't really expecting an answer.

"I'm not in the mood right now," A-K told her trying to avoid an argument because no matter when he came into Keba's beauty salon he and Mini would always end up arguing about nothing.

"Nigga, I just asked you a question," Mini said not letting what A-K said intimidate her.

"Bitch, I said I'm not in the fuckin mood!" A-K shouted.

"Like I always say, ya bitch is what you rode in this world on," Mini threw back his way.

A-K pulled out his gun and pointed it at her. "You gonna make me fuck over yo tired ass," A-K said with the gun pointing straight at Mini's head. She certainly wasn't backing down now because of A-K's gun pointing at her.

"Them hoe's you fucking tired," Mini said looking A-K straight in the eyes when she said it.

"Fuck you, hoe. Reach me ya car keys, YoungOne. I'ma go sit in the car before I—" He was cut off by Mini.

"Before you what?" Mini responded letting A-K know she was not scared.

He just shook his head and walked out. YoungOne and Power-Up was just sitting there laughing hard off what just took place.

"What the hell so funny, Power-Up?" Mini asked laughing herself.

"Girl, you throwed off fuckin with A-K like dat," Power-Up said.

"You know he's crazy," YoungOne pitched in.

"Fuck him, I don't say nothing when he start with me," Mini explained.

Jam came out the office hugging one of the people he loved more than life itself. Keba and Power-Up caught eye contact, but it seemed much more like a look of 'I want you so badly.' Straight up, love was going through their bodies.

"Well, lil sis, we bout to roll out," Jam said as he kissed Keba on the cheek. Keba walked over to where YoungOne was, gave him a hug, and told him Tatianna, a chick hair she be doing, was asking about him. Then she walked over to Power-Up and gave him a hug so welcoming that they could feel each other's heartbeat.

"Damn!" Power-Up knew it sounded like Keba moaned when she hugged him, he thought to himself. After Keba finished hugging Power-Up, she looked around for the other one. "Where's A-K?" she asked.

"Mini pissed him off so he went sat in the car," Power-Up answered.

"Those two always at each other throats," Keba said and walked towards the door to wave goodbye to A-K. When Power-Up was walking out the door Keba asked him when he was gonna stop by again and for YoungOne to get at ole girl so she could leave her alone. Jam stopped, he and Keba exchanged a few words then he walked to his truck where his dawgs was waiting on him.

CHAPTER TWELVE

On the other side of town, Boo told his crew to start their jobs ASAP. Buck said he would start his mission tomorrow getting his car washed. Bouncy needed a haircut real bad, so he also said he would go get a cut tomorrow and see what was going on in the barber shop. Then, Seven said the quicker all of'em could come up with some money the sooner he'd be able to start peeping out the gambling shack. Finally, Boo agreed to go peep out Keba's Salon in two days.

After leaving the beauty salon, the Gutta Boyz drove to TJ Ribs to get something to eat and discuss business. Jam said he needed to run something by them. Sitting at a table for four, A-K seemed like he was in another world.

"A-K that shit gonna get handled," Power-Up said meaning the niggaz who shot at him earlier.

"Dat shit fuckin with my brains, Thug. Just let me know when I be slipping hard. I saw my whole life flash right in front me. Them fools must pay for scaring me like dat," A-K explained with a very deadly look in his eyes.

"You still here, baby, so let's order some food and get our grub on. Like you said, you was slippin and whoever wanted yo head didn't capitalize," Power-Up said.

"But, we gonna capitalize off them niggaz for shooting and missing," Jam said then called the waitress to let her know they ready to order.

"How can I help you handsome guys," the waitress said.

"I'd like the Baby back ribs special," Jam said flirting with the fat waitress.

"Give me the BBQ wings," YoungOne said then asked A-K what he wanted because he had his head down on the table. "Whatever you ordered," was the reply A-K gave back, and then he placed his head back on the table. Power-Up also ordered the BBQ wings.

"Bring some wine coolers back if you don't mind," Jam said winking his eye at the waitress making her feel good to be flirted with. Once the waitress walked off Jam built up the guts to tell his lil brothers bout the changes he was about to make.

"A-K, you need to chill the fuck up, dude. Long as you stay in dat mind frame you gonna run round here like you in a cowboy movie—pop, pop, pop!" Jam said acting like he had a gun in his hand making gunshot sounds.

"I don't know how you know dat's what's on my mind because I know who that was tried to take me out," A-K said with dat devilish grin he does when he thinking evil.

"Well, who it was then?" YoungOne asked ready to go retaliate.

"The fool I shot in Dixie," A-K explained. "Since I been thinking bout it, that clown was stunting."

"The nigga shot ya car up, A-K, how the hell was he stunting," Power-Up stated getting mad at A-K for feeling like a nigga always stunting.

"Man, when I looked up and seen the gun pointed out the window, dude coulda took my head off but guess what? Nigga shot the side of my car up. Not the window where I was but the back window," A-K said with a serious look on his face.

"How you know it was dude you shot in Dixie?" Jam then asked.

"I just know dat's who it was. Now, what you had to discuss with us Jam," A-K said changing the subject. The waitress came back with the food and wine coolers then placed each of their plates in front them. She set the wine coolers on the table and said, "If y'all need something, just call out."

Jam dug in his pocket, pulled out a hundred dollar bill and handed it to her then thanked her for the service. The waitress also thanked him for breaking bread then walked off twisting her over size hips. Jam started eating his food trying to get his thoughts on how to break the news down about leaving the game.

"I been wanting to holla at y'all bout the changes I'm bout to make," Jam said sensing each of them looking at him with his face in his plate.

"Like what?" YoungOne asked with a concerned look thinking Jam was talking about how they were handling business.

"Man, I been in this game a long time and now I'm married with two kids that I wanna see give me grandkids," Jam was choking with emotions in his voice as he said that.

"What you trying to say, Thug?" Power-Up asked not liking the sound of Jam's words.

"If y'all stop interrupting me, maybe I can finish," Jam replied. But, on the cool he was happy that they kept cuttin him off because he really didn't wanna tell 'em it would be over for him soon. He went on anyway to get it all over with.

"Well, in a few days y'all know I take that ride to re-up. I'm bringing Power-Up along on this one so he can meet the connect because this is all over for me," Jam finally laid it all out. A-K was about to say something but Jam stopped him so he could finish talking. "I made a lot of money in this game. I can really say the game been good to me so far, and I would like to end it on that note. Y'all know I'll always be a Gutta Boy 4 ever. I just wanna do the family thang now. I'll always be here for y'all no matter what. I will still hang out sometimes. All my shops and click houses I'ma split with y'all. I'ma be legit. I want y'all to always remember this game don't last forever. Right now y'all can walk out this with me if y'all want."

"Power-Up, A-K, and YoungOne stopped eating their food and looked at Jam with the same expression like, "hell nah."

"I figured y'all wouldn't wanna leave the game right now. But, I understand," Jam said. Power-Up was the first one to say something about the whole situation.

"Big brother, I feel where you at," he said.

A-K grabbed his wine cooler then looked toward Jam. "I don't understand it but I gotta respect it," A-K said.

YoungOne just shrugged his shoulders as if saying whatever.

"When the time comes we must have a going away party at the strip club," Power-Up said.

Jam then grabbed his wine cooler and looked around the table at each one of his dawgs then said, "Let's toast to that."

"I'd love to stay with you niggaz all day but I gotta go get myself ready to take some twins out to eat tonight," Power-Up said rubbing on his chin.

"I feel dat cause I'm trying to get at this lil broad I met last week," YoungOne threw out there letting his boyz know he was bout to bounce out too.

"In four days, Power-Up, we gonna take that ride," Jam said as he stood up and placed another hundred dollar bill on the table.

"Well, since I don't have one of my cars right now, Jam, drop me off at home to get one," A-K said.

"Keep ya eyes open brother," YoungOne directed at A-K giving him pound then did the same with Jam and Power-Up before he left. Power-Up slapped hands with A-K and Jam before he left to go chill with the twins.

Boo was sitting in his car thinking bout which one of the gutta boyz shop they should hit first. These clowns won't know what hit 'em. He wished they could hit all the spots they had but that wouldn't be necessary once they got that nigga Jam. Boo was getting excited thinking about how he was bout to start balling when a junkie knocked on his window trying to buy a hit of crack.

After leaving TJ Ribs Power-Up went straight home, took a quick shower and was lying back when he received the phone call he'd been expecting telling him to meet them at Copeland's. When he hung up the phone, he went to his closet, looked through his wardrobe, and decided to put on a Polo outfit with his Polo boots. He studied himself through the mirror a few times then hauled ass to see if he could have the pleasure of twins, something he had yet to accomplish. The night spot the twins had chosen was on Coursey Blvd. which was where you'd find many ballers taking in the night life to spend a lil fetti and take on some of the most beautiful women you'd ever see.

He entered Copeland's and immediately seen it had been a busy night with the crowd inside. Power-Up spotted the twins sitting in the back but had to do a double take because they looked totally different from the last time he seen them.

"Hey, ladies," he said as he approached the table where they were sitting. He was smelling and feeling like a big dawg. Their response was a simple smile but the looks in their eyes said it all. They wanted him as bad as he wanted them. He sat down at the table and they all ordered something to eat and drink. As the night went on they began to get more loosened up and he learned they were some gutta ass bitches. They were born and raised in Baltimore, Maryland. They finished high school and went to college. Meka, the oldest by three minutes and eighteen seconds, graduated as a dermatologist while Mecko, took up paralegal studies to be a lawyer. To pay for themselves through college, they soon found themselves dancing in strip clubs to provide and support themselves. One night they received news while on campus that their mom and dad had died in a car accident. Being the only two kids and twins made them stick together by each other's side. After they received their degrees they decided to travel from state to state until they found that right man for the both of 'em. That's the kind of life they wanted, to never be separated.

Dealing with so many different kinds of men in their lives had taught them a lot. Before they knew it, they were in the game hustling niggaz and jacking niggaz. The longest they ever stayed in a state was six months at the most and then it's off to another one. If they wanted stop doing the thangs they do to hustle niggaz, they had enough money to do it.

Power-Up kind of believed them but he wanted to know why they was telling him all this shit. He was beginning to feel like 'where was all this shit heading' and what they trying to tell him? Or maybe it's just the wine that had them both tipsy.

"Power-Up, out of all the men we done met and had dealing with, and this our thirteenth state, we really like you. I guess it's the confidence you have. It's like demanding and your swagger is one of a kind," Mecko said looking Power-Up in the eyes with those pretty brown eyes of hers. All Power was thinking then was well, 'I demand some pussy right now' but decided to save those thoughts until later on.

"I think we may stick around for a while if you can handle that. But, tell us something about yourself, Power-Up, starting with your real name," Meka said looking so damn seductive.

Power-Up went on and told them his name Keith, he'd just gotten out of prison, and he had three dudes who all three was like brothers to him, and they're known as the 'Gutta Boyz'. They wanted to know how he was getting money. He just told them what they don't know want hurt them, but that what he's eating could hold them down in all ways. They seemed to be satisfied with his response and rolled with that. Then Power-Up asked. "What's y'all real names?"

"Shameka and Shamecko," Meka answered. They excused themselves to the ladies room but only Mecko came back asking was he ready to leave. Power-Up went with the flow and said he was then got up to pay for the food and drinks. She wouldn't let him though, saying if he paid for the food he could stay here by himself so he obliged. She said Meka was waiting in the car. Power-Up was feeling like these hoes trippin with the pussy until Mecko followed him to his car and got in the passenger side then said. "Follow her."

YoungOne was riding around talking on the phone to the lil chick he met walking home from school. "Can I pass by your house," YoungOne asked her thinking the answer would be "no."

"Why you wanna pass by my house?" came the response.

"I just wanna come see you," YoungOne said.

"Pass by the school the same time tomorrow. I'll be walking again," LaShay said.

"I need to see your beauty tonight," YoungOne threw back at her hoping that would do it.

"Since you said it like that, I guess you can," LaShay told him.

"What street do you stay on?" YoungOne asked excitedly.

"Charles Street. I'll be sitting outside, and don't take all night to come because I do go to school. I don't have it like you," she said.

"Don't say it like that because what I got you can have," YoungOne threw at her with feeling in his voice.

"I'd rather have my own, but thanks for the offer," LaShay said smiling to herself.

"What side of Charles Street do you stay on?" YoungOne asked happy that she was allowing him to pass through.

"Right off Winnbourne on the curb," LaShay replied.

Being only five minutes away, YoungOne knew she wasn't outside so he decided to wait until she'd be on the street she lived on before he asked her if she was outside yet.

Power-Up knew one thang—it was bout to go down with these two bad bitches. He had to find out do they fuck with ecstacy so he pulled out a purple blunt and asked Mecko riding with him do she smoke. "No, we don't do drugs," she responded.

Power-Up knew then he had to slip the x-pill on them so he asked Mecko, "do y'all wanna stop and get a daiquiri?"

"I don't care it's all on her. You need something because you seem kind of nervous," Mecko said while smiling.

"Nah, I'm good. Just want something to sip on," Power-Up said. Mecko then grabbed her cell phone and called her twin sister who was following and asked her do she wanna stop and get a daiquiri. Power-Up was saying a silent prayer that she'd say 'yes.'

Mecko turned toward him and said, "Meka said if that make you have a lot of stamina she cool with it." Power-Up shook his head with a grin on his face thinking in his mind 'only if she knew.'

"Tell her I'ma pass her up so she can follow me," he told Mecko to relay the message. She told Meka what time it was then hung up the phone.

"What color yo house is?" YoungOne asked as he approached the block.

"Blue," LaShay responded.

"You stay on side DJ 'nem then?" YoungOne asked but knew the lil nigga his future wifey stayed next door to. He knew 'em from the game. They was doing major thangs like him in the drug game. "Well, I'm sitting outside waiting on you," YoungOne said. Bout three seconds later LaShay pulled the curtains back looking out the window. "You coming out?" He asked her while still talking to her through the phone.

"You see me?" LaShay asked waving her hand standing at the window.

"No, I want you to come outside. These niggaz next door already just standing there staring at my car," YoungOne told her. She opened the door and walked outside toward his car when one of the niggaz must've spoke to her because she waved and kept walking toward the car. YoungOne got out then leaned against the door.

After they hit the daiquiri shop and was riding again Power-Up asked Mecko. "Where are we headed?" He was feeling curious all of a sudden. He remembered these twins just told him how they jacked niggaz from other states.

"To our nice two bedroom apartment," Mecko said. Then she begin to explain to him about every nigga they introduced to their home be the chosen one for them until he fuck up somehow or don't fit their criteria as the relationship goes on. "So, Power-Up, are you ready to share two women at one time all the time?" Mecko asked matter-of-factly.

"I can handle it," Power-Up stated back looking at her with a playful frown on his face, which was letting her know he could handle it and some.

"You fuck with, or used to fuck with, one of them niggaz over there?" YoungOne asked soon as LaShay made it to where he was standing.

"You ask a lot of questions for somebody who just came to see a person," LaShay said with a smirk on her face that attached him immediately.

"I'm not worried about them or nothing else. I only like to know what I'm facing," YoungOne told her also with a smirk on his face.

"No, they're just my neighbors. Been that way since I moved here five years ago," LaShay told him. After chillin with LaShay until her mom came home from work, which was two hours later, he was feeling good as a mutha fucka like he had fucked her, but it was only 'QT,' quality-time. He was still thinking about LaShay as he was driving across the river to pass by Club Vibe to see if he could find a freak to take to the hotel for the night.

Power-Up was watching Mecko closely to see if the x-pill had started to take effect. When they made it to the daquri shop he went in and walked to the counter where a lil freak named 'Shorty Red' worked and handed her three fifty dollars bills. "Hook up three power-ups," he told her. She already knew he was talking bout three daquri with pills mixed in it.

From the look of it the pill was beginning to work on Mecko by the way her mood changed from laid back to hype. They was still following Meka's car. They followed her to Sherwood Forest neighborhood then pulled in the apartment complex's security check-point and continued following Meka until she pulled in front apartment number ninety-eight. They pulled up next to her. She was just sitting in her car with the music playing, snapping her fingers and moving her head in circular motions.

Power-Up knew the pill had taken effect on her. Mecko jumped out the car walking toward their apartment door, stuck her key in, opened the door and started undressing right there until she was standing in the door with just panties on. Knowing it was bout to go down Power-Up lit up his purple blunt, took a hit, grabbed one of his x-pill and chewed it up then got out the car.

Meka was getting out her car at the same time. She walked over to where he was still sippin on the daiquiri and grabbed his hand and led him inside their apartment. Once inside, she took him to one of the two bedrooms where a big king size bed was waiting.

"Make yourself comfortable, and please be naked when we return," Meka said walking off swaying her hips.

Power-Up stood there watching her go and thinking to himself which one of 'em pussy he wanted to eat first. Looking around the bedroom he noticed a picture frame and knew off top it was the twins' parents. From the beauty of the lady, they looked just alike, to the height and complexion of the man on the picture.

As Power-Up was staring at the picture he felt r someone else behind him.

"Meka said she told you to be naked, I see you don't follow instructions," Mecko said as she snuck up behind him. He ignored her remark for the time being.

"These y'all parents?" Power-Up asked her instead.

"Yes, now give me this," she said grabbing the picture, kissed it, then laid it face down on the night stand. "You want me to help you undress or you gonna do it yo'self?" Mecko questioned.

Power-Up was so into checking things out around the apartment that he didn't realize she was naked until she walked off to the closet door, bent over, and started digging in a gym bag. The girl pussy was looking like barbeque chicken bent over like that. Real fuckin delicious.

Mecko stood up and turned his way with a camcorder. "You wanna make a movie?" she asked then pointed the camcorder at his dick. "Look like somebody is excited," she said then began sticking her finger in her pussy. "Get undressed," she demanded moving closer to him. Meka walked back into the room looking the same as her sister with nothing on. Power-Up decided to speed up the process by taking his clothes off in less then five seconds. He was standing only in his polo socks and his dick pointing straight at them crooked as a mutha fucka.

"Lay back on the bed," Meka said as she got finished kissing and swapping spit with her sister. He quickly backed up to where the bed was and laid down in the middle of the bed. Meka grabbed the tropid stand and adjusted it at the foot of the bed. She then got in the king size bed and started crawling toward him. Mecko set the camcorder down on the night stand and she, too, started crawling toward him like a tiger. Meka sat on his face with her's facing the camcorder. Mecko started sucking his dick and that shit was feeling better than government cheese. He raised Meka off his face to see why Mecko stopped when he didn't feel her mouth on his dick. Mecko just looked at him then reached under the bed and came up with a shoe and poured all the contents on the bed.

"What the fuck you bout to do with that shit?" Power-Up asked her seeing all types of dildos and other sex toys. She grabbed the silver bullet, stood up then bent over and started back giving him knowledge.

"Why you stopped?" Meka asked him reaching for the silver bullet her sister had in her hand. He had to see what the hell was going down in this bitch. Prison made him a freaky ass nigga but not that fuckin freaky to take shit up his ass because that's what he was thinking at the moment these two hoes had in mind. Until Meka started playing with Mecko pussy from the back while she was slurping on his dick.

Power-Up started back eating Meka pussy for another twenty to thirty minutes as if she was made of candy. Meka and Mecko were so gone on them x-pills freaking each other out that they forgot about him. So, he just sat back at the head of the bed and started beating his dick watching them go at it like two pit bulls fighting. Mecko grabbed a strap on dildo as Meka positioned herself doggy style while Mecko began pounding her pussy walls out. Power-Up couldn't take beating his shit no more. He eased behind Mecko and inserted his dick in her wet pussy, found the strokes she was giving her twin and went to work.

"Aaaahhhh. Baby, fuck meeeee! Mecko was screaming. Meka was saying shit and he didn't understand a word of it. After a while of that oral love making, Meka and her twin switched positions, and he finally skeeted. Power-Up was so drained when he nutted that he just lay still completely content. The twins lay down beside him, one in each of his arms and fell asleep.

CHAPTER THIRTEEN

One week later, Boo was ready to move on the first plan. He called his clique and had 'em all meet up in Prescott where he'd soon be running with an iron fist.

Laying back on some real low key shit, trying to find the niggaz who shot up his car had A-K feeling like a buster. This is what he was thinking that as he rode through the Bottom. He needed to hit the club tonight, but first he wanted to check and see if his lil brother would wanna roll, too. A-K dialed YoungOne number up.

"What's up?" YoungOne answered.

"Chillin. Trying to see if you going out tonight," A-K stated.

"I don't know," YoungOne replied.

"Man, what you mean you don't know. You been acting funny with a nigga all week. I know what it is," A-K said mad at his dawg.

"Nigga stop acting like a fucking broad. I'll never act funny with you. What you rolling or something, getting all emotional and shit," YoungOne said knowing A-K get soft-hearted when he full of them x-pills.

"Yeah, I'm rolling but that's not why I feel like that," A-K said back.

"I'ma go with you. Where you going?" YoungOne asked sensing the sad tones in A-K's voice.

"Don't worry bout it bruh. Go chill with lil Barbie," A-K said then hung the phone up.

Jam guessed it was really meant for him to get up out the game because everything went sweet with Power-Up meeting the connect. On his last re-up they made it back safely. In two weeks he was hanging his jersey up. Jam was in deep thoughts thinking while he hit blocks through EasyTown with the lil freak Renada's head buried between his legs.

That nigga A-K was trippin on some shit. How dat fool can say I'm acting funny? Fuck, YoungOne thought. He'd just been putting in work with girl. Maybe I am on some not hollering at him shit. Let me call my dude back before he start shooting people up, he was thinking but at the same time dialing LaShay's number instead of A-K's.

"Ahhh shit," YoungOne said pressing the end button on his phone. He then called A-K.

"What's up?" A-K answered after letting the phone ring for a few seconds knowing it was YoungOne calling.

"Say A-K, you on some dumb shit. Nigga, you know where we stand. I'm just feeling girl. Don't ever feel a hoe can come between us," YoungOne told A-K.

"I know YoungOne, I'm just trippin. I feel like putting that tool on a nigga," A-K said laughing.

"Nah, chill with dat shit dude," YoungOne replied in a serious tone then asked, "now what club you going to?"

"L.A.-Live," A-K answered.

"I'ma meet cha there," YoungOne said.

"Aight," A-K replied.

"One," YoungOne said.

"One," A-K said back then hung up.

Since the twins worked tonight, Power-Up thought he'd drive out to White Castle and hit Club Runt to see what was poppin. No, he changed his mind because he forgot bout the two tickets to the LSU women's basketball game. He could use a female athlete on his team to fuck. After all, he was Power-Up.

Everybody had made it to the meeting so Boo laid out what they was gonna hit first.

"This how we gonna do it. We gonna have two cars which are right there," Boo explained pointing at two rock renters. "We gonna park on side of Lincoln Theater, which sits on 13th Street and walk next door to the barber shop. Bouncy, you gonna sit in the car that you and Buck will be in because they know you now from getting yo haircut. You gonna have the choppa with you. Anything goes wrong come through the door blasting. We have three hours to chill. Let's go get something to eat, on me," Boo said walking to the Chinese store where they sell fried turkey wings.

Keba decided to say fuck it. She needed some loving tonight. Not that she ain't been getting none. Her old man been giving her pleasure but tonight she needed something different. And only one man can fulfill her desire at the moment. Sitting in her office she finally built herself up to make the phone call. But, what will she say to Power-Up once he answered? She was thinking that while sitting in her office looking at the picture on the wall. It's just like the one she carried around in her purse. The phone was ringing and she was just about to hang it up until the caller said, "Hey, Keba."

"Hey, Power-Up," she responded.

"What's up?" Power-Up said after the phone went silent for a few seconds.

"You and Jam 'nem together?" Keba asked.

"No, I'm just riding around killing time before I go to the LSU women's basketball game," Power-Up said.

"Who going with you?" Keba asked hoping not another female or none of the Gutta Boyz. Maybe she could have a reason to like basketball.

"Actually, I'm going by myself, but I do have two tickets. You wanna go or you don't like sports?" Power-Up asked.

"I would love to go. I ain't doing nothin," Keba said happier than a punk in a dick factory.

"Game start at 7:30pm. I'll pick you up at 6:45, so where you gonna be at the Beauty Salon or at home?" Power-Up asked.

"I'ma be at home. I'll just let Chocolate Thunda close the shop," Keba answered already gathering her things up to leave.

"OK. See you then," Power-Up stated.

"Alright, I'ma be waiting," Keba responded.

"One," Power-Up said then hung up.

All week these niggaz been giving YoungOne stares everytime he pulled up. He felt like there was gonna be some trouble before it was all over with. YoungOne grabbed his 45 caliber, stuffed it in front of his pants, and got out his car.

"Who you looking for?" One of the niggaz next door to LaShay's house asked.

"Not you," YoungOne replied getting mad at the nigga for the semi-check play.

"We don't let niggaz come back here messing with our hoes," a different dude said.

"Nigga, you playing with me?" YoungOne asked while reaching under his shirt for his gun.

"Hey, what's going on?" LaShay asked after opening the front door and seeing the anger in YoungOne.

"Nothing," YoungOne replied as he walked on the porch to go inside.

Jam had dropped the lil freak who was giving him brains off in McDonald's Land. On his way home he stopped by his sister's shop. He pulled up on side of Keba's car while she was bout to pull out. Jam rolled down his window to see what the rush she was in was all about.

"Hey, baby sis, what's up? I see you in a rush," he said.

"Yes, I'm on my way out," Keba said trying to cut through the chase. Keba mind started playing tricks on her because the way her brother was looking was like he knew who she was gonna be with. "Well, not out to no night club," Keba continued.

"Ok, enjoy yo'self. I'll catch up withcha later. Love you," Jam said before rolling up his window. Jam grabbed his purple blunt and lit it up so he could stall time to let his sister pull out. He was really contemplating following her to see why she was acting so nervous. Instead, he pulled out and headed home.

After getting off the phone with YoungOne, A-K drove to the Mall of Louisiana to just walk around even though he knew he would end up leaving with bags.

"What they said something to you?" LaShay asked YoungOne when he made it inside.

"They playing with the right one," YoungOne said before giving her a kiss on the lips.

"They just jealous because they trying to holla at me and I don't give 'em a chance," LaShay said smacking her lips.

"Fuck them, I came to see how my baby doing," YoungOne said smiling and showing all twelve of his platinum teeth with the crushed diamonds.

Boo and his clique was getting ready because they only had an hour left before it all went down.

Power-Up couldn't believe he asked Keba to come with him to the game. Ain't no telling what might happen. His dude is everything to him and going against his word would be very disloyal, Power-Up thought while checking himself out in the mirror. Seeing that his Adidas fit was straight he put on his platinum chain with the platinum cross hanging from it. He sprayed some Badazz cologne on and headed out the door to pick up Keba.

A-K had made it to the mall and was bout to get out his car without his strap. But, something kept telling him to get it, so he grabbed his 44' Magnum and stuck it in his pants then walked in the Mall.

Keba had made it home and took a quick shower. She didn't know what to wear so she settled for a pair of faded dark blue baby phat jeans with the baby phat v-neck top to match. Keba was happy she decided to get her finger nails and toe nails done clean the day before because her 6 inch dark blue Jimmy Choo heels maked her the right height for Power-Up. She was looking at her butt in the mirror when her cell phone started ringing.

"Hello," she answered.

"I'll be pulling up in front of your house in bout five minutes," Power-Up said on the other end of the phone.

"Alright, I'm ready," Keba replied.

"One," Power-Up said before hanging up.

Keba put on her lip gloss with the light blue tint in it. Then, she put her necklace with the letter "K" in diamonds on, and grabbed her Jimmy Choo clutch purse and shades. She almost forgot to spray a lil of her new fragrance she brought from New York last month. Keba sprayed on some Escada Ocean Lounge and headed out the door where Power-Up was waiting after blowing his horn.

Walking through the Mall of Louisiana, A-K always felt was a good way to ease stress because the majority of times he would end up pulling a bad bitch or buying some new clothes and shoes. After hitting foot locker for three pairs of tennis shoes, he headed to the jewelry store to check out some jewelry. As he was walking out the jewelry, store he felt a pair of eyes on him. Ever since his car got shot up, he'd been on point—always watching his surroundings. The growl of his stomach made him realize he hadn't eaten since this morning. He caught the escalator to the McDonald's, and ordered his favorite, a double meat cheese burger, large fries, some BBQ sauce instead of ketchup, and a strawberry milk shake. He was deep off in his burger when again them same set of eyes walked through the door and straight to his table. A-K grabbed his 44 and placed it in his lap. There were three of 'em and he didn't recognize none of 'em from no incident in the past.

"You know Tara?" the nigga that walked with a limp asked.

After thinking about who dat was A-K responded, "why?"

"Because that's my girl, and I seen yo picture in her phone," the nigga dat walked in first said.

A-K looked at dude and started laughing. The niggaz acted like they were bout to charge A-K up until he showed them that big monster. A-K placed his gun on the table and then looked at dude hard before asking, "is she worth dying for?"

The nigga seemed to have come to reality and started backing. While he was backing up A-K put him on top of game. "Don't check me dude, check your hoe," A-K said then grabbed his bags and walked out the Mall before he caught a case in public.

Keba came strutting out the house looking excellent. She must've known Power-Up liked to see a woman with lip gloss on. He got out his car and walked around to the passenger door and held it open for her.

"You look beautiful," Power-Up said when she made it to the car.

"Thank you," she responded back.

He jogged back to the driver side, got in, and then pulled off. He handed Keba his CD case. "Find something to listen to," Power-Up told her.

"I'm cool with what playing," she said.

"What made you call me because I'm curious to know that," Power-Up asked her off top.

"Nothing in particular, I was just thinking about you at the time," she said very smooth-like.

"Don't say it like dat," Power-Up replied looking at her shaking his head.

"It's only the truth," Keba responded, batting her eyes. Power-Up didn't want to hear no more because they wouldn't even make it to the game. He just left it at dat.

Them niggaz got my nerves all fucked up. I'm glad you came outside because ain't no telling what was bout to happen," YoungOne was saying to LaShay while she was doing some homework.

"Don't let them get to you, you hear me YoungOne?" LaShay asked.

"Uh huh," YoungOne responded.

"Then promise me that," LaShay said looking at him and waiting on him to reply.

"That's a promise I can't make. But, I will try," YoungOne said being real.

"Why? You not good at keeping promises?" LaShay asked then turned all the way around on the couch to face YoungOne.

"I'm good at keeping my promises but not that one. I promised to be your man and treat you like a queen," YoungOne said looking LaShay up and down.

"You're a hot mess," LaShay said smiling.

"I gotta go meet with A-K. I'ma pick you up from school tomorrow," YoungOne said as he stood up to leave. LaShay walked him to the door where they hugged and gave each other a soft kiss. YoungOne walked to his car thinking the niggaz was waiting on him but to his surprise, they were gone.

CHAPTER FOURTEEN

Driving with Keba in the passenger seat felt like right. Power-Up took a peek between her legs when he pulled in the LSU parking lot, and from the looks of it, that pussy was fat. He wanted to ask her so bad, "can I eat that between yo thighs?" But, he kept his thoughts to himself.

The game was packed tonight. It's always like that when LSU played against Tennessee. He found a parking spot and they got out the car. Power-Up walked to the front of the car where Keba was waiting, grabbed her hand and headed inside the Pete Maravich Center to show off a bad bitch with him.

They made it inside to their seats in the fourth row. "Which one you like?" Keba asked as soon as they sat down. He thought Keba asked that question because of the way was he was looking at LSU shoot-around.

"LSU," he said back.

"I know that. I'm talking about which player?" She asked with her heart touching smile.

"Oh! The one with the dreadlocks. She the female Jordan," Power-Up answered pretending like he was shooting a basketball.

The Hittin Licks Clique was all set to do the damn thang. Boo started explaining how they was gonna get in the shop and snatch the nigga C-Mo who Bouncy said run it. Plus, they planned to take whatever everybody else in there had, too. They would try to be in and out in ten minutes. The quicker they finished, the quicker they could hit the other one.

YoungOne called A-K to let him know he had made it to the Club. A-K let him know he was also on his way. After leaving LaShay's house, YoungOne didn't bother to go home and change clothes. He just went straight to the Club and into the VIP section.

A-K had gone home and put on his red monkey outfit with a pair of his new King James tennis he brought from the Mall earlier. He pulled in the Club parking lot, found YoungOne's car and parked next to it. Before getting out he grabbed his bag of x-pills then headed inside.

The game had just started with Tennessee winning the tip.

"Wanna eat some of them good hot dogs and popcorns?" Power-Up asked pointing at the dude walking around selling refreshments.

"I'm down for whatever you wanna do," Keba said letting him know that he was in control. That last statement caught Power-Up totally off guard. He ignored it and beckoned for the food servant man. Tonight's game was gonna be a high scoring game. Four minutes had pass and the score was already twelve apiece. The food servant had made it to where they were. Power-Up ordered six hot dogs, two bags of pop-corns, three drinks, and two cotton candies.

"Damn, baby, you hungry, huh?" Keba asked shaking her head and smiling at the goodies he bought.

"This is for me, and you," Power-Up said laughing too.

Boo and his clique pulled up on 13th Street and parked the renters where he said they would park. Boo, Buck, and Seven all were dressed in different color hoodies with ski masks on their heads, which they would put right on before they entered the shop.

They got out the car. Boo told Seven and Buck to wait until he saw what was up and told Bouncy to be on alert. Then, he walked clean by until he was out the sight of the niggaz inside. He stopped and gave the hand signal to Buck and Seven to move in. Once they was close enough by the door, Boo placed his ski mask on and the three of 'em bum rushed the barber shop.

"Lay it down!" Boo shouted pointing his sawed off shot gun at the niggaz standing around. Buck and Seven had their big monsters pointed at the niggaz cutting hair. Boo spotted the nigga C-Mo who Bouncy said ran the shit from the chain on dude's neck, which read 'Mo-C' spelling his name backwards.

"All you mutha fuckas put ya hands on y'all fuckin heads," Buck commanded. All the niggaz in there followed the orders and did what he said. Buck handed Seven his glock-nine millimeter and started searching all the niggaz and customers for guns. Out of the six niggaz who was working in the shop cutting hair, four of 'em was strapped. Buck moved to the three niggaz who was getting haircuts and searched them, too, and one of 'em had a gun. Satisfied, he received his glock back from Bouncy.

"Lay that apron on the ground," Bouncy said to one of the niggaz. Boo, seeing that his clique was handling shit good, decided to take C-Mo, Mo-C, or whoever he was to the office to see what was up.

"Don't you run this place?" He asked looking at C-Mo.

"Yeah," dude replied with no fear in him.

"Let's go see what's back there," Boo said pointing at the closed door sitting off from where they cut hair. "Anybody sneeze, shoot'em," Boo told Buck and Seven then walked off with his sawed off pointed at C-Mo's back.

YoungOne was chillin in the VIP section with his mind on LaShay. He got up and walked to look out at the crowd and spotted his brother A-K squeezing on a hoe name Iesha's ass who had tattoos of butterflies on several parts of her body. He grabbed her hand and headed up to the VIP section. YoungOne really didn't feel like dealing with no hoe at this moment. But, knowing them two freaky mutha fuckas was on their way upstairs, he had to find somebody to keep him company.

"What's up, brotha?" A-K asked when he made it to the VIP area.

"Everything's good," YoungOne answered.

"Hey baby," the freak Iesha said grabbing YoungOne's dick.

"Chillin," YoungOne replied.

"I get to have both of you to myself again?" Iesha asked no one in particular. A-K turned and walked off to the table where the drinks were to see which one he wanted.

YoungOne fell in pursuit with Iesha on his heels. A-K popped the top on the Grey Goose and turned the bottle up to his mouth.

As soon as he finished quenching his thirst, he asked YoungOne and Iesha, "y'all rolling?" then pulled the bag of pills out his pocket.

"Of course," Iesha pill-headed ass answered first.

"I'm straight," YoungOne said.

A-K got one of the double stacked pills called 'superman' out the bag then looked at the freak.

"Want this one in yo booty hole?" he asked Iesha.

"Fuckin right," she said with no hesitation and started pulling her low cut Roc-a-Wear pants down.

Keba had eaten half a hotdog, some popcorn, and half of her cotton candy. She was enjoying herself, watching Power-Up eat all that stuff like wasn't no tomorrow. She knew that was how that shit would have him and her brother 'nem whenever they be smoking.

"I'm good now," Power-Up said.

"I hope so," Keba said laughing.

LSU stole the ball and went down court and scored a layup. The crowd went wild when LSU blocked Tennessee's point guard shot then went the other way with the ball. Number 23 was standing in the corner when the ball was passed to her, and she knocked down a three pointer. Tennessee called time out to calm LSU's players and fans down.

"You enjoying the game?" Power-Up asked Keba.

"Yes, I didn't know it be like this at these games," Keba responded looking around at all the people and signs they were holding up. She reached over and kissed him on the cheek.

"What's dat for?" He asked looking her in the eyes.

"I don't know. I just felt like doing it," she said looking back at him in a very seductive way.

"You act like you scared of me, Power-Up?" she said, looking as innocent as can be.

"Why you say something like dat?" Power-Up asked.

"That's the vibe I be getting when we around each other," Keba said lowering her voice.

"Trust me, I'm not scared of you," Power-Up responded.

"I can't tell. I know you see how I look at you whenever I see you," Keba said looking out toward the basketball game.

"You know what's up, Keba?" Power-Up asked.

"No, I don't, so please tell me," Keba said turning her head toward him waiting on his response.

"Jam," Power-Up said looking in Keba's eyes.

"Forget, no, fuck Jam!" Keba shot back. After LSU went on a six to zero run with two minutes and twelve seconds left before half time, the crowd went up in all types of roars again.

"That door locked?" Boo asked C-Mo.

"Nah," he answered. They made it to the door and C-Mo opened it up.

"Turn on the lights," Boo commanded standing back off the door in case dude decided to try something. C-Mo hit the light switch to his right and the lights came on. Boo then moved inside.

"I'ma ask you this one time only, where's the money and the work at?" he said in an aggressive voice.

"This all I got," C-Mo said walking behind the desk in the office. Boo wanted to make sure dude didn't try anything so he followed him to the desk. C-Mo came up with what looked like a half kilo.

"Set it on the desk and walk over here," Boo demanded. C-Mo walked to where Boo was standing with his hands held up.

"Now turn around," Boo said. As soon as he turned around Boo struck him over the head and he fell face first to the floor. He made sure C-Mo was out cold then closed the door and started searching. A few minutes of tearing shit up, he found a pound of purple and a half pound of regular weed. Boo was standing in the middle of the office looking around trying to figure out where they would hide shit at in there when the door opened. Buck walked through with his gun pointed and ready to blast.

"What's up man," Buck asked.

"I think I'm forgetting to look somewhere. Hold this," Boo said handing his sawed-off to Buck. He started knocking the pictures off the wall to see if they had secret spots behind them. After he finished, he headed back to the desk and got down on the floor on his back.

"Bingo," he said coming up with two lil silver boxes. He unlocked one of the boxes and it was filled up with money and different kinds of pills. When Boo opened the other one, it only had stacks of money inside. Buck was looking around for something to put the work in when he spotted a brown box closed up.

"Get the box," Buck said pointing his gun in the direction. Boo ripped the box open and came up with two gallon jugs. He opened the top and sniffed the jug. A big smile spread across his face.

"What?" Buck asked.

"Got us some dranks. This shit is syrup," Boo said excitedly. Buck tucked his gun in his pants so he could have a better grip on the sawed-off. Boo packed everything in the box and once it was finished he and Buck walked back to the front where Seven was still holding shit down. Boo stopped and grabbed the apron off the floor with everybody shit in it and placed it on top of the box. The Hittin Licks Clique walked out like nothing happened. They made it to the rock renters where Bouncy was waiting with both cars running.

"Mission Two," Boo said to his clique then threw the box and the rest of the stuff in the back seat of the car he was driving.

After A-K stuck the pill in girl's ass, he handed her a different one with a gun on it to pop.

"I'll be back," YoungOne said walking out of VIP. YoungOne saw a lil hoe named Crystal he used to fuck when he was like 14 of 15 years old. She was 18 years old at the time with an old man. But, she loved herself some Young One.

"Hey Chester," YoungOne said creeping up on girl. Crystal turned around happy because she knew only one person ever called her that--a term referring to a child molester.

"Hey, my baby. How you doing? I ain't seen you in a long time," Crystal said looking YoungOne up and down.

"I been making it," YoungOne replied.

"From the looks of it, you doing big thangs," Crystal said checking out his platinum grill and the ice on his neck and wrist.

"I'm chillin up in the VIP section if you wanna chill up there," YoungOne said, at the same time grabbing her hand.

"You and A-K still cool?" she asked.

"Yeah, he up there in the VIP section," Young One responded.

"I see a lot of things look different since I moved to Shreveport," she said.

"Uh huh. You left me to go give dat pussy to them up north niggaz," YoungOne said grinning at her.

"You know it wasn't like dat. I had to leave dude. He turned into a woman beater," Crystal said as they made it to the VIP spot.

"Let's take a bathroom break while it's halftime," Power-Up said then took Keba's hand in his.

"Where we going after the game?" Keba asked.

"Wanna take a walk downtown? That's real relaxing," he said trying to avoid an argument bout him being scared of her.

"I told you I'm down for whatever," she said letting him know ain't no limitations. Then she looked at him and asked, "How you feel about me, Power-Up?" as she stood by the bathroom door.

"Why you doing dat, Keba?" Power-Up asked before he walked into the men's restroom. He was taking a piss when he reached for his phone on his side to see if anybody called. Because of all the noise in the place, he couldn't hear it. But, it wasn't on his side!

"Fuck," he said to himself mad, "I lost my phone."

"You talking to me young brotha?" The older black dude in the bath room asked.

"Nah. I'm talkin to myself," Power-Up responded.

"Long as you didn't answer yo self," the older man said before washing his hands and leaving out. How I'ma end this night with her? She on some other shit. Keba want me to put dat pound game on her. His thoughts were interrupted while washing his hands when the bathroom door opened.

"Thought you ran off and left me here," Keba said standing in the door.

"Nah. I'm on my way out now," Power Up said turning around to walk

Keba moved in for the kill. "I was really coming to see if you needed any help," she said seductively while grabbing his dick and sticking her tongue in his mouth at the same time. They fell off into a cold blooded saliva exchange.

"Excuse me," the white man said standing in the door. "Sorry to disturb you guys but my son has to use it real bad," he explained.

"It's ok," Keba replied then walked out. Power-Up had to take a few seconds to recuperate before walking out behind her.

Boo had already explained before they left Prescott about the two licks. The first one was accomplished. Now it was off to the second one. He would be sitting in the car on this one. "Call Bouncy," Boo said to Seven handing him his cell phone.

"What's up," Bouncy answered on the other end.

"Put the phone on loud speaker and tell them to do the same," Boo told Seven.

He related the message through the phone. "Ya'll hear me?" Boo asked.

"Yeah," came the response.

"Same thing we just did. Only I won't be in there. So, Bouncy, you find Keba and see what's in dat office. Like I said ain't no work in there, but its money in there. Y'all make it quick, ya feel me," Boo said.

"Aight," Buck and Bouncy said through the phone.

"You can hang it up," Boo said to Seven. Then he turned to Seven, "Don't shoot nobody," he warned.

"I'm not unless they trip out," Seven said looking at his 357 magnum.

"For real dude. Them females not gonna trip, but they might do a lot of screaming and shit. So yeah, they might trip but they want try nothin," Boo explained to give Seven trigga happy ass a better view of the situation.

Jam made it home before his wife and kids. He took a quick shower and decided to take his family out to dinner. His kids wanted to go to Chucky Cheese, and they all agreed on going to the movie theater also. After completing the family-night-out-thang for the pass hour and a half, he was finally at home laying across the bed massaging his wife's feet. They both were enjoying the moment when his phone started ringing.

"Hello?" Jam answered.

"Man I been trying to catch up with Power-Up," the caller said in a panicked voice.

"I talked to him earlier today. What's up?" Jam asked.

"Nigga stuck the shop up about fifteen minutes ago," dude said on the other end.

"I'm on my way. Keep trying to call Power-Up," Jam replied.

"Aight," C-Mo said.

"Did they still have niggaz getting haircuts?" Jam asked.

"Yeah, four of 'em," C-Mo answered.

"You called the police?" Jam then asked.

"Nah. I wanted to see what Power-Up wanted to do," C-Mo responded.

"Good. Don't. I'll be there in twenty minutes. One," Jam said then hung up.

His wife was sitting up in bed looking sad because she knew their moment together was ruined. But she understood the position her husband held in the game. She just hoped he got out before it was too late.

"Love you baby," Jam said then gave his wife a kiss before leaving.

YoungOne and Crystal made it inside the VIP section. Iesha was dancing off dat 'Lollipop' by Lil Wayne while A-K was sitting back rubbing his dick. He looked up and seen girl with YoungOne, he couldn't believe it was Crystal. She was a bitch he wanted to fuck when he was younger but she started giving YoungOne dat pussy. Even though he and his dude shared hoes she never was game for it.

"Hey, A-K," Crystal said walking over to give him a hug.

"What's up, Crystal?" A-K replied back then stood up to hug her back. Iesha stopped dancing and just stared. She was feeling like 'this bitch all in my way,' because she wanted a train ran on her tonight like the other times before.

A-K seen how Iesha was standing there looking, so he introduced her and girl hoping they could do a switch-'o-roo tonight.

"You drink?" A-K asked Crystal.

"Yes," she said looking around, "what y'all have?" she asked.

"Grey Goose, Hennessey, and some Remy. If you want something else, we can make it happen too," A-K responded.

"The Grey Goose straight," Crystal replied.

They was all chillin getting their drink on when YoungOne asked A-K "where's the Jigga's at?" A-K handed the pills to him. YoungOne chose a blue dolphin double stack. "You roll?" YoungOne asked Crystal.

"Sometimes," she said back. He needed to hear no more. He found a yellow one with a spaceship on it and handed it to her. She accepted it then chewed it up. A-K watched with excitement because now he had a chance to fuck dat pussy til it fart.

YoungOne's phone started vibrating on his side. "What it do my nigga," YoungOne answered knowing who was calling. "He's right here," YoungOne said looking at A-K.

"Aight. We on our way," he said to the caller.

YoungOne explained to A-K that it was Jam, and he wanted them to come to Power-Up's Barber Shop cause some niggaz just laid it down.

"Y'all chillin with us?" A-K asked Crystal and Iesha.

"I am," Iesha said looking at Crystal.

"I guess I am, too," Crystal said looking towards YoungOne.

"We gotta go check something out first, so let's bounce out," YoungOne said as he and A-K got up and left.

Boo 'nem had made it to their second destination. They pulled up in the abandon building parking lot next door. Boo looked at the cars in the parking lot of the Beauty Shop to see who was all at work. "Damn, she not here," Boo said out loud.

"Who?" Seven asked curiously.

"Keba, the bitch who own the place," Boo responded.

"Fuck her," Seven said. Boo got out the car and went told Bouncy Keba wasn't there and to just kick in her office door and search her shit.

"Aight," Bouncy replied.

"Let's roll," Buck said.

"Bring yo phone Bouncy because if Keba pull up I'ma call you," Boo said.

"Cool," Bouncy responded aftergetting his phone putting it in his pocket. The Hitting Licks Clique ran behind the abandon building they was parked by then came up on side the Beauty Shop. Only Boo stayed behind the building with the choppa in case those gutta boyz clowns pop up. Bouncy, Buck, and Seven had made it close to the front door. Bouncy was making hands signals counting, and letting them know on count of three. The women in the shop was so busy shoo-shooing they never saw it coming. The three of 'em bust through the door with Bouncy leading the way.

"Nobody fucking move," Bouncy demanded. All the women was in shock seeing niggaz masked up with guns in their faces.

"Make this easy and do as we say," Buck replied. There were the four women who work in the shop plus the two who was getting their hair done. "All y'all move over there," Buck said pointing to the wall. The six women moved to the wall with no problem.

"Put cha hands on y'all head," Bouncy said as he reached Seven his gun. He then searched all the women to make sure they didn't have a gun or knife. Buck grabbed the apron off one of the chairs and laid it out in front the women.

"Put everything y'all have on that," he said pointing with his gun at the apron. All the women started taking their jewelry and everything out their pockets throwing it on the apron.

"What you waiting on?" Seven asked the one wearing the chain that said 'Mini.'

"Fuck y'all. I ain't giving up shit," she responded back with tears in her eyes.

"Oh, you wanna make this hard, huh," Buck said.

"Girl do as they say," one of the other women said.

"Ya'll some sad ass niggaz. Coming in here robbing a bunch of women," Mini said crying.

"Bitch shut up, and do as we say. I won't ask you again," Seven replied walking towards her.

"This not worth dying for Mini. Think about your kids," another woman said.

"Fuck them pussy," before she could finish her statement Seven had whopped her across the head with his gun. The women started hollering at the top of their lungs.

"Shut the fuck up," Seven demanded. He then took Mini's jewelry and everything out her pockets.

"Come on man," Bouncy said to Seven then turned and told Buck, "hold it down in here. I'm gonna go check out the office."

"Aight," Buck replied.

Seven kicked in the door of Keba's office then he and Bouncy started searching like they were two hound dogs looking for a nigga who escaped from prison.

Power-Up and Keba had made it back to their seats. The game had already begun when she started her investigation soon as he put his attention back into the game.

"You never said how you feel," Keba said bringing him back to their previous conversation.

"Chill with that," Power-Up responded back.

"What you scared of Jam?" she persisted.

"You know I'm not scared of no nigga," Power-Up said getting mad at Keba for trying to play mind games.

"We both grown and if you feel about me how I feel about you, then nobody can stop us from being together. Unless, you don't feel how I feel," Keba said looking in Power-Up's eyes.

"You crazy girl," he said smiling at her.

"About you." she shot back.

Bouncy and Seven had torn Keba's office up and came up empty handed. Only thing they found so far was a big gold ring with a 'K' in the middle surrounded by diamonds. That, Seven slipped into his pocket without saying anything on finding it.

"Let's go," Bouncy replied. They both went back to the front where Buck was with the women. Seven grabbed the apron off the floor and they walked out. Once outside, they all hauled ass to the cars and pulled out in the night wind.

YoungOne and A-K had made it to the Barber Shop with the two hoes following behind them in their own cars. Ain't no way they was gonna let Crystal get away without smashing her. Jam was standing inside talking to C-Mo when they walked in. As soon as they made it to him he asked, "Ya'll seen or talked to Power-Up?"

"Earlier," YoungOne responded beginning to feel something serious went down.

"He probably laid up, or at the Strip Club," A-K suggested.

"I took care of the niggaz who was robbed in here," Jam said to A-K and YoungOne.

"What they hit for?"A-K asked.

"C-Mo said twelve grand, a pound of purple, a half a brick, and a half-pound of regular weed, nine hundred pills, and two gallows of syrup plus the shit they took from the dudes who was getting their hair cut. Just a slap on the wrist," Jam finished.

"We'll find out who it was, believe that. And when we do," A-K said grabbing his glock kissing it.

"Let's keep trying to call this nigga Power-Up," Jam said.

Keba's phone was vibrating one her side. She never looked at it. Instead she just sent it straight to her voicemail. A few seconds later it started vibrating again. This time she looked at the number and seen it was Yoshi calling. "Bitch this better be damn important calling me while I'm trying to get me some," Keba said whispering so Power-Up couldn't hear her. But, all Keba heard over the phone was crying and Yoshi trying to say something.

"I can't understand you," Keba said.

Yoshi pulled herself together and told her they just got robbed by three dudes and that one of 'em hit Mini across the head with his gun. When Keba asked her did she call the police that got Power-Up's attention. He started asking her what happened while she was still on the phone. Keba hung up the phone then looked at Power-Up with a strange look on her face that he could tell something was wrong.

"We gotta go. Niggaz just robbed my shop," she explained. They both got up and rushed out the stadium bumping into people on the way out not even giving a damn. When they made it to the car Power Up opened the door and spotted his phone on the driver's seat vibrating.

Boo and his clique had made it back to Prescott. They all went up to his apartment to split up everything. "Even though we ain't got too much from them hoes, we did straight on the barber shop hit. It might be a change of plans on the Detail Shop and gambling shack. They may be on the alert now. Ya feel me," Boo said to his boys.

"Man this ain't shit. I still wanna hit the other two," Buck replied.

"I said change of plan on robbing the other two because of this. Let's just nap dat fool Jam and get some real gorilla bread," Boo responded.

"I'm down with that," Seven said rolling up some of the purple they just hit for.

"Ya'll down with that?" Boo asked to Buck and Bouncy.

"All the time," Bouncy replied.

"Long as its money, ya know I'm bout it bout it," Buck answered also rolling up some of the regular weed they hit for.

Picking up his phone and seeing Jam's number, Power-Up thought he was calling to tell him bout the Keba incident. "What's up Thug?" Power-Up answered when he picked up the phone.

"Where the fuck you at? We been trying to call you for a minute now," Jam asked pissed off.

"At the LSU game," Power-Up answered. Keba was sitting in the passenger seat frowned up not only for her shop being hit, but also the way Power-Up was acting nervous on the phone which meant one thing. He was on the phone with her brother.

"Well, man your cousin C-Mo called me when he couldn't get in touch witcha. Three dudes hit yo shop," Jam explained but didn't hear any response so he asked, "What's up?"

"You ain't gonna fucking believe this shit," Power-Up began saying.

"What?" Jam asked quickly.

"I brought Keba to the game with me and she just got a call from Yoshi saying three niggaz ran in her shop," Power-Up said.

"You and Keba?" Jam asked curiously.

"Yeah, I'll explain later," Power-Up replied.

"Everything straight over here. I'ma meet cha at Keba's," Jam said then hung up.

"Why you looking like dat?" Power-Up asked Keba.

"I can tell you was on the phone with Jam because how nervous you was acting," Keba said looking out the car window.

"Keba chill with that shit right now. Something going on," Power-Up said.

"Why you say dat?" she asked.

"Jam said three dudes hit my shop in the south, too," he told her. They rode the rest of the way to her shop in silence.

"I just got off the phone with Power-Up, and he's on his way to my sister's shop. One of the girls who works there called her and said three dudes robbed the shop," Jam told A-K, YoungOne, and C-Mo.

"Niggaz trying us or something," YoungOne stated.

"Let's go see what's up at Keba's," Jam said to A-K and YoungOne, gave C-Mo pound, and then left. A-K and YoungOne stopped and hollered at Crystal and Iesha before going to Keba's Shop. They agreed on sending the two women to the hotel to wait on them there.

On his way to Keba's Jam called all the other shops to make sure everything was ok then he let them know what happened and to be on alert for shit. After he finished dat, his thoughts went to Power-Up and Keba at the game. That's what he said. Then why wasn't he answering the phone? I see why she was acting so nervous today when she said she was just going out. I know my dude ain't playing me like dat. Jam was so gone in his thoughts dat he didn't realize his phone was ringing.

When they made it to the shop and walked inside it seemed like the women were in shock. Seeing Keba they all stood up and walked over to her crying and trying to say something at the same time, leaving the police just standing there. Keba and Power-Up just hugged the women trying to comfort them. Yoshi started explaining everything dat happened including Mini being taken to the hospital. The police finished their questioning then left. Keba walked off to her office with Power-Up following behind her.

"I wonder what are they was looking for." Keba asked out loud to herself.

"Whatever they could find," Power-Up answered for her.

"I gotta go see Mini," Keba said walking back to the front of the shop where the other girls were. Then Jam,

A-K, and YoungOne came in running through the door.
Jam walked over and gave Keba a hug whispering in her ear
telling her everything gonna be alright. He then looked
over at his dude Power-Up and gave him a crazy look.
They gave each other hard stares until Power-Up walked
out the shop.

"What the fuck was dat about?" A-K asked Young One
seeing the looks his dawgs was giving each other.

"Yo guess is as good as mine," Young One replied.

Power-Up was sitting in his car contemplating what
to do next seeing all the women leaving the shop. Only
his boyz and Keba was left in there. So he picked up his
phone and called Jam.

"What's up?" Jam responded when he answered the
phone.

"Come outside," Power-Up replied. Jam walked outside. Power-Up got out the car when he saw Jam approaching then said, "what it do, thug, and what was the
look all bout inside?"

"Dude, all that I have given you I never asked for shit
in return but one thang from you, A-K, and YoungOne—
not to fuck with my sister," Jam responded with an angry
tone.

"She called me just to holla. I had two tickets to the
game so I asked her did she want to go with me," Power-
Up said trying to explain the situation.

"Where y'all was going after the game?" Jam asked.
Power-Up was standing there dumbfounded and didn't
know what to say. He was starting to feel kind of guilty because he knew how he truly felt about Keba in his heart.

"Exactly what I'm saying is this, what were your intentions after the game was over?" Jam demanded after Power-Up didn't respond.

"We was gonna go downtown and take a walk," Power-Up finally answered.

"I see. Y'all on a romance kick behind my back," Jam said with his fists balled up.

"That's all I was gonna allow to happen," Power-Up replied.

"It was meant for y'alls shit to get hit, or something worst woulda happened," Jam said.

"You blowing shit out of proportion," Power-Up said backing up a little in case Jam decided to swing a punch at him.

"You ever seen that movie Scarface? Dats how I feel about my sister dude!" Jam said with beads of sweat popping on his forehead.

"Nigga I'm fuckin loyal to you. If I wanted Keba I coulda been had her. The realness and love I have for you wouldn't let me do it," Power-Up replied back, getting pissed by the minute.

"That's whatcha say," Jam said never taking his eyes off Power-Up.

"You tripping bruh," Power-Up said turning around to go get in his car.

Keba decided she'd clean up her place tomorrow, but for now, she had to see what was going on between Jam and Power-Up outside. She went stood by the door where A-K and YoungOne was watching her brother and his dawg argue. They were trying to figure out what was going on, but she knew what was going on between them two outside, or at least she had a feeling.

"I'm bout to go," Keba said to A-K and YoungOne. They all walked outside. YoungOne and A-K walked towards Jam to see what was going on. Keba stopped and turned to lock up her shop. Then, she started rushing towards them when she heard Power-Up start his car up to leave. "I'm bout to go see Mini at the hospital," she said, waving her hand at Power-Up to wait for her. When she made it to where her brother 'nem were standing, Jam just stared at her without responding.

Keba kissed him on the jaw and told him to be there for seven o'clock in the morning. She then hugged YoungOne and A-K and strutted off to where Power-Up was waiting in his car.

"They think I'm fuckin stupid," Jam said looking at A-K and YoungOne. "I'ma get at y'all tomorrow," he said walking off to go get in his car.

"What he said?" Keba asked as soon as she sat down in the passenger seat.

"Nothin," Power-Up replied.

"You mean to tell me y'all stood out there in a real serious mood and talked about nothin?" Keba responded back.

"Know this Keba, I won't let a woman come between me and my dawg," he said. Her body tensed up when he said that.

"I didn't ask you to. Furthermore, you can take me home to get my car. I can drive myself to the hospital," she said turning her whole body around to face the car door window.

"I'ma take you. What hospital Mini's at?" Power-Up asked, but she kept facing out the window. "I can drive all night until you tell me," Power-Up stated.

"The General," she finally answered after a few minutes realizing he was serious. "He's not my daddy. I'm 24 years old. I'm fuckin grown," Keba said out loud.

"He knows you a grown woman. He always told us that you was off limits to the crew," Power-Up explained.

"You not understanding," Keba replied.

"I do. I also understand where he coming from. Jam knows what type of nigga I am," Power-Up said tapping her on the head.

"Don't touch me! What type of nigga are you then?" Keba responded with asking.

"A Gutta Boy," Power-Up answered.

"Well, I'm in love with one," Keba said in a soft, trembling voice.

Everybody was straight after Boo split all the shit up they hit for, and some of his clique was ready for some more action. "When we gonna get this nigga Jam?" Buck asked Boo.

"I already been peeping out how he roll. It's kinda hard trying to get to him because he never take the same route every day," Boo explained to his crew.

"Dat fool can be got," Seven said.

"Anybody can get it," Bouncy threw in.

"All I'm saying is why waste time chasing him when we can just wait at his house for him," Boo responded.

"You know where dat clown stay at?" Seven asked.

"I know a lot about dude and his wife," Boo stated.

"How and when is we gonna get at him then?" Bouncy asked.

"We gonna snatch his wife and two kids. She always picks the kids up from her mama's house at 4:30 in the evening. I watched her ever since we started watching the shops," Boo said.

"So we gonna do it tomorrow?" Buck asked but not really looking for an answer.

"Give me a lil more time to check thangs out and I'll let y'all know when the time is right. Until then let's have fun off what we hit those fools for already," Boo replied.

"I'm bout to go to the club," Seven said.

"Fuck it, why don't we all go together," Boo stated. They all agreed on going to Club Top of Line because they keep some fire ass shit going on. Then, yo status had to be somewhat right. If you was at that club you was doing straight. And Boo and his crew was feeling like ballers at the moment.

CHAPTER FIFTEEN

YoungOne and A-K was still standing in the parking lot of Keba's Salon when A-K's phone started vibrating. It wasn't until after seeing ole girl number when he realized he had forgot they sent Iesha and Crystal to the hotel. "What's up?" A-K said answering his phone.

He and Iesha exchanged a few words then he hung up the phone and said to YoungOne, "They're waiting on us in room 220 at the Ramada Inn."

"Aight," YoungOne said.

"You not going?" A-K asked hitting the power button on his car keys to make his Chrysler 300 come to life.

"Yeah, I'm rolling. I'm just trying to figure out what's up with Jam and Power-Up," Young One replied.

"I think Keba played a part in it," A-K suggested.

"Dat's what I'm thinking. I know Power-Up ain't violated the man sister," Young One said.

"We'll find out tomorrow. Now, let's go dog these freaks," A-K responded.

They walked off and hopped in their whips then drove to the Inn.

Riding around with all kind of crazy thoughts going through his mind, Jam decided to hit the club, something he stopped doing a few years ago. He pulled up in the club parking lot and parked. Deciding on whether or not he should leave or go inside he said fuck it and got out then walked in straight to the bar.

"Hey, stranger," the lady bar tender said wearing a pink G-string set.

"What's up, Lexis?" Jam spoke back.

"What bring you out in this environment tonight?" she asked.

"Need to take my mind off something right now," Jam responded.

"I get off in another hour if you want some company," Lexis said.

"I'm cool with dat. I'm going up to VIP section. Send me some Henny and coke up there," Jam told her before walking off.

"Baby, I'm in love with you, too. The first day I seen you when you came to visit Jam in prison it was love at first sight for me," Power-Up said expressing his feelings toward her.

"Because of Jam we could never be, that's whatcha saying?" Keba asked wiping her watery eyes.

"You just thinking about you and me. Dat's gonna always be your brother no matter what. Niggaz don't meet too many dudes like Jam so when you does you cherish dat, ya feel me?" Power-Up said trying to get through to her.

"Whatever," Keba responded. Power-Up was happy they had pulled up at the hospital to end the conversation.

Before the car had stopped all the way, Keba opened the door and got out. She started walking toward the entrance doors.

Boo and his clique was chillin in VIP section with four nice females. They was taking turns ordering bottles of Dom Perignon really getting their stunt on trying to impress the women they were kickin it with. Boo, seeing how the females was treating them like they was ballers, made him want to get money for real. If only they could hit it big whenever they caught up with Jam. After tonight, he would start stacking his paper off the work they hit for because he was feeling like it was his time to shine. His thoughts were cut short by one of the females licking his neck. Then, that's when he saw him walking in the VIP section next to theirs.

YoungOne and A-K had made it to the Inn and went up to the room where girl 'nem was waiting. A-K knocked on the door.

"If y'all don't have big dicks, please leave," Iesha said through the door.

"We have enough," YoungOne responded.

"Can y'all last?" she shot back.

"Long as I have these jiggas, we can last all night. Now open the door," A-K said.

Iesha opened the door with just her thong on. When they walked into the room, Crystal was laying across the bed in her shirt and panties.

"Can I have some of that?" A-K asked Crystal, seeing her laying in a sexy pose.

"You still with the foolishness, huh?" Crystal asked but was looking at YoungOne.

"It's cool, Crystal, Young One don't mind," A-K replied.

"I hear you," she responded.

"So, are we sharing or what?" A-K asked her again.

"I need another pill," Crystal said.

"I guess dat mean it's going down," YoungOne said.

"Why are y'all still dressed?" Iesha asked them. YoungOne started undressing in a heartbeat. A-K handed Crystal another pill then passed one to Iesha and YoungOne. Then he chewed one. In seconds, he was standing in his boxers. Crystal took her shirt and panties off then opened her legs to the max exposing the inside of her pussy.

YoungOne climbed on the bed between Crystal's legs and buried his head between her legs. In the other bed, Iesha sat down at the end of it and started giving A-K head.

"Hold on," Crystal said making YoungOne lay on his back then she lay on top of him in the sixty-nine position. A-K was enjoying getting his dick sucked by Iesha, but he wanted some of Crystal.

"Come on," A-K said to Iesha pulling her head off his pole. He wanted to see if Crystal was down for whatever.

"Go sit in his face," he said to Iesha. A-K walked to the bed where YoungOne and girl was then told Crystal to turn around. She just looked not knowing what was going on. YoungOne pushed her pussy out of his face because once he seen Iesha climbing on the bed by him he knew A-K wanted Crystal.

A-K grabbed Crystal by the hands and eased her off YoungOne. Iesha, not caring what the fuck was going down, hurried up and sat on YoungOne's face. It wasn't like it was her first time with them. He turned her backside toward him and made her climb back on the bed and started back sucking Young One dick. A-K guided her body to form a hump in her back then he started looking at her from the back. After he couldn't take no more, he started eating her virgin looking pussy.

Young One moved from under Crystal sucking his dick and placed Iesha in his spot to see if Crystal was gonna eat Iesha. "What?" she reacted when Iesha laid there.

"Eat her," Young One said.

"I never did dat before," Crystal replied making fuck faces from A-K still eating her pussy.

"A first time for everything," YoungOne responded. Crystal was so gone off them pills that she wasn't caring about doing anything. She dove off into girl pussy like a pro. YoungOne got on his knees in the front of Iesha and rubbed his dick on her lips.

Power-Up and Keba had went inside the hospital and saw that Mini who was doing well. The doctor wanted to keep her over night to run some more tests on her because of the hard blow she took to the head. Her family and kids showed up, so Keba and Power-Up hugged her and promised they'd be there first thing in the morning. They pushed out to give her family time with her.

Keba stormed back to Power-Up's car in a mean but sexy walk. Knowing that he was watching she put an extra twist in her walk. She stood by the passenger door waiting on him to unlock it. Since she was acting crazy, Power-Up walked straight to the driver's side, got in, and hit the switch to unlock the passenger side door. Once she was in the car, he pulled off. He was looking out the corner of his eyes to see the reaction on her face from him not opening the door for her.

"You wanna stop and get something to eat?" Power-Up asked.

"I want you to speed up ten more miles and drive me straight home," Keba shot back rolling her eyes all in one motion. He reached over and started tickling her trying to get her to lighten up a little.

"Stop touching me," Keba responded giggling softly. She grabbed his CD case and put on Mary J. Blige, then leaned her seat back and relaxed her mind until they pulled up in front her three bedroom brick house.

Jam was sitting in the VIP section drinking like it was his last day living. He was thinking bout what Power-Up said. He wanted to believe him, but he knows how dudes are. All his life, he always wanted the best for his only sister, and he knew being with Power-Up would bring pain to her life.

"You alright in here?" Lexis asked as she walked in.

"I'm good, lil mama," Jam responded.

"You still want my company?" she asked sitting down on his lap.

"Why wouldn't I," Jam replied squeezing on her ass.

"Looks like somebody happy already," Lexis said rubbing on his dick.

"You gonna take care it for me?" Jam asked placing light kisses on her back.

"I'll be your slave tonight, do dat answer your question?" she replied.

"Well, we're wasting time in here," Jam responded.

"Yes, we is," Lexis said standing up to leave.

"Where we going?" Jam asked.

"Wherever," she answered.

"The room," Jam said standing up. He downed his drink then he and girl busted out.

Not wanting to alert his clique, but he couldn't believe this fool was in the VIP section next to them. Boo was pissed off seeing Jam acting like what they got robbed for wasn't fading him. The way he was smiling and touching on the fine ass bartender made him wanna get at dude sooner than he planned. The DJ came on the loud speaker asking all contestants to report to the main stage. Tonight, Club Top of Line was having a Shake Dat Ass contest, a Who-Wear-A-Thong-Better contest, and the Most Prettiest Pussy contest.

"It's bout to go down," Boo said to his boys. Even the women jumped up to go be spectators. No matter if it was men or women, everybody liked to enjoy the shows. Boo took his mind off Jam and headed outta VIP to go enjoy himself.

Tired of getting his dick sucked, YoungOne pulled Iesha from under girl head. Iesha gave him a cold stare.

"Come on," YoungOne said walking to the other bed. He grabbed a condom out of his pants pocket on the way to the bed. He stood at the end of the bed and placed the condom on then bent Iesha over the foot of the bed and started busting her pussy up.

A-K had finally stopped eating Crystal. He being the type of dude who hateed using protection, even though the rate of H.I.V. was high in Baton Rouge, he felt like condoms took away too much of the pleasure. So he crawled on top of Crystal and stuck his rock hard piece in girl. She was feeling so horny she never asked about protection either.

"You on the pill?" A-K asked meaning birth control.

"Uh huh," was all she said enjoying the sensational feeling she was having.

A-K and YoungOne switched girls several times until A-K couldn't go no more, and that's how the night ended for him. But, YoungOne still had more energy left. He went took a shower with the two freaks and had a threesome. After that he couldn't go anymore either. He was done, too. They all came out of the shower together and he stopped and laid on the floor. Girl 'nem moved back to the bed and went at it some more. He watched until he fell asleep like A-K was doing.

"You coming inside?" Keba asked. Power-Up was sitting there not knowing what to do or even how to answer her question. He didn't want to hurt the feelings of a woman who had his heart.

Keba got out of the car and stood by the door. "Whatcha gonna do?" she asked again.

"I don't know, Keba," Power-Up replied.

"Boy, come on. I ain't gonna do you nothing," she responded closing the door and walking off. Power-Up grabbed his gun from the seat and followed her inside not knowing what the temptations might bring on.

When he made it inside, Keba had already hit the button on the remote. R. Kelly's 12-play CD was blaring through the surround sound system.

"Make yo'self at home," Keba said walking off into one of the back rooms.

He was looking through her DVD movies collections when Keba came back in the living room. Seeing what he was looking at she asked, "See something you wanna watch?"

"No, I wasn't trying to find anything. I was just checking out all the movies you have," Power-Up answered. He turned around to face her now, and his heart skipped several beats. She was standing there with her hands on her hips wearing a pair of short-shorts, which hugged her pussy, a white t-shirt with no bra, showed her nipple prints as clear as day.

"Want something to drink or eat?" Keba asked leaning against the wall.

"What do you have to drink?" Power-Up asked turning back around looking at the DVDs to get the evil thoughts out that running in his head.

"Basically, whatever you want. You know I have a liquor cabinet for whenever I have guests visiting," she responded.

"Cristal would be cool," Power-Up replied.

"Find us a movie to watch," she said before going to fix his drink. He wanted to make sure he found the right movie for them to watch. He didn't want to look at no love movie or one with strong sexual acts in it. He found 'Bourne Identity,' which was perfect. She came back with a drink for him, and she was sipping on one herself.

"I didn't know you drink," Power-Up said with a surprised look on his face.

"I sip sometimes," she responded smiling.

"Here," he said reaching her the DVD. She looked at the DVD and frowned. He knew she wouldn't like the choice of movie he gave her, and it showed in her facial expression.

"What?" Power-Up asked.

"Nothing," she replied turning the stereo down and putting the movie in the DVD player. Power-Up took a seat on the all black leather sofa. Keba walked off and came back with a pillow and a blanket. She set her drink down and laid the pillow on Power-Up's lap, then put her head down on it, and covered herself up with the blanket.

Jam gave the bar tender two-hundred dollars and told her to go to the Hilton.

"Where you going," she asked.

"I gotta go handle something. I won't be long. Text me and let me know what the room number is," Jam told her.

"I'm going to the one on Perkin Road," Lexis said.

"Aight," Jam said then headed toward his car. He drove across town to see if he was wrong, but when he made that left turn and cruised pass all the brick homes he saw what he didn't want to see. He pulled off, burning rubber and running stop signs, not giving a fuck. At the same time, he was feeling betrayed by two people he had mad love for.

Seeing what he just saw made him lose all of his desire for girl that was headed to the room. He turned his car around and headed back to the row of brick houses. When he made it in front of the one he was looking for he turned the ignition off and waited.

A-K woke up and lit up the purple blunt he had in his pocket. "YoungOne!" he called not seeing him in the bed with the hoes. "YoungOne!!"

A-K said louder thinking he must be in the bathroom. YoungOne never answered so A-K climbed out of the bed. That's when he saw him lying on the floor buck naked.

"Man, get up," A-K said shaking YoungOne with his foot.

"What time is it?" YoungOne asked with his eyes still closed.

"Seven-thirty," A-K responded.

"Aight," YoungOne said. He got up and lay down in the bed with Crystal and Iesha.

"We gotta go see what's going on with the shit that happened with Jam and Power Up," A-K stated. YoungOne's mood and his mind was still dealing with the shit from last night, but he got up and put his clothes on. A-K was doing the same thing. When they finished getting dressed they left without saying a word to Iesha or Crystal who were both dead to the world.

"Call me when you get straight," A-K said.

"Where you on your way to?" YoungOne asked.

"The same place you going—home," A-K answered.

"Aight," Young-One said.

"I'ma call Jam on my way home," A-K said getting in his car. YoungOne dialed his baby's number hoping she wasn't busy in school. Fantasia was playing on her ring tone for a few seconds.

"Hello," she said when she answered.

"Hey baby, I just wanted to hear yo voice," YoungOne told her.

"If that's whatcha say," LaShay answered.

"For real boo, I don't wanna interrupt you from getting yo "edumucation." But, I'm still coming to pick you up," YoungOne told her.

"I hear ya," LaShay responded.

"I won't be late," Young One replied before hanging up.

On his way home, A-K pulled up to the drive-thru of McDonald's to get some breakfast. A-K had forgotten that he told YoungOne he was gonna call Jam until he saw the lil hoe Jam put him on one night at the window. A-K and the broad shot the breeze then she gave him his food with extras. He pulled off then called Jam.

"Where this nigga at?" A-K thought to himself after Jam's phone rung until his answering machine picked up on his cell phone. A-K called back because he wanted to know where they were gonna meet. Finally, he answered as soon as A-K was bout to hang up.

"What's up?" Jam said in a low tone.

"Man, you still sleep?" A-K asked.

"Something like dat," Jam responded.

"Where we meeting at?" A-K asked.

"Say A-K, I might do something I may regret in the long run," Jam said in a calm voice not even answering the question A-K asked.

"What cha talking bout thug?" A-K asked sensing shit wasn't right.

"Always live by loyalty," Jam said then hung up. A-K immediately called Jam back but got no answer.

Power-Up woke up laying behind Keba on the sofa with his arms wrapped around her. He laid there trying to remember taking his shoes off and laying in the position he found himself in. His mind couldn't register back to the episode. But laying there with an early morning hard on felt damn good the way Keba had her ass backed up on his tool. She made a sudden move that made his dick come to life for real. Power-Up hurried up and climbed from behind her before shit got out of hand.

"Where you running off to this early?" Keba asked. She'd been woke the whole time enjoying the semi-hard on Power-Up had. That's the reason she moved her ass up and down a few seconds before because she knew he was woke.

"I gotta go," Power-Up said walking off to the bathroom.

"I thought you were going to see Mini this morning?" Keba asked loud enough so he coul hear her from the bathroom.

"I'ma drive over there, what time you going?" Power-Up responded back asking her.

"I thought we was going together," Keba said walking toward the bathroom door. Power-Up took a piss, washed his hands, cleaned the morning dew out of his face, and rinsed out his mouth. He stepped out the bathroom to find Keba standing right there.

"Keba, I can't have you with me all day. I gotta find out about them robberies last night. And I gotta see what's up with yo brother, ya dig," Power-Up explained. Keba stood in front Power-Up and started rubbing her temple.

"Bye," she replied.

"Walk me to the door," Power-Up said putting his arm around her neck. They made it to the doorway, he gave her a kiss on the cheek, and turned around to leave. That's when he spotted his boy's car in front of Keba's house with him sitting in it just staring.

Jam got out of his car with his forty-five in hand. That's when Keba saw Jam walking towards Power-Up.

A-K called YoungOne and told him what Jam said to him. YoungOne said he would try and call him. A-K said he was bout to call Power-Up to see if he knew what was going on with their dude. He called Power-Up and his phone was ringing then it went to his voice mail. YoungOne was getting the same treatment from Jam so YoungOne pressed the end button and started dialing A-K's number, but A-K was on the line already.

"Hello," YoungOne said hearing a voice on the phone calling his name.

"What the hell you doing?" A-K asked.

"I was calling you. How the fuck you get on the phone?" YoungOne questioned him back.

"Because I called you, nigga," A-K replied.

"Oh, you got in touch with Power-Up?" YoungOne asked.

"Nah. I guess you didn't get in touch with Jam neither?" A-K asked.

"No," YoungOne responded.

"Well, I'ma ride by Keba's when I get situated so call me when you get straight," A-K said.

"Aight," Young-One replied.

"One," A-K said.

"One," YoungOne said back then hung up the phone.

Seeing the evil look in Jam's eyes, Power-Up didn't know if he should run or stay because he realized he'd forgotten his gun beside Keba's sofa. So, he settled for staying where he was.

"This how you play me dude?" Jam asked when he reached where Power-Up was standing.

"It ain't what it seem, my nigga," Power-Up responded. By this time, Keba was making her way to where they were.

"Be a fucking man and tell me you went against our loyalty for each other," Jam said.

"Man, I told you ain't nothing going on with us," Power-Up responded.

"Dude, you fucking stayed here all night and you gonna stand here and tell me nothing happened," Jam concluded. Keba made it to where Jam and Power-Up was. She stood there listening and got tired of Jam with his accusations.

"I can handle myself, Jam. I don't need you worrying about if he stayed here or not. I'm not a lil girl, okay! So stop treating me like one!" Keba screamed.

"You need to go back in the house, Keba," Jam responded.

"I need for you to get out my yard with that gun in yo hand," Keba replied.

"I oughta kill you right now," Jam said ignoring what his sister was saying as he looked at Power-Up.

"Don't threaten me dawg, " Power-Up warned.

'Fuck you! I ain't cha dawg," Jam said raising up his gun. Seeing Jam point his gun at him, Keba quickly stepped in front of Power-Up.

"Dude, I'll disregard the fact that you got yo gun in my face, but you going too far," Power-Up said without blinking an eye.

"Get the fuck out my yard," Keba said walking up on her brother. Jam raised his gun in the air and let off all seventeen shots then looked at Power-Up and said, "You a snake dude."

Keba was standing in place crying and screaming for Jam to just leave. After empting his clip Jam walked off, got in his car, and put the pedal to the medal. Power-Up made his way to Keba and placed his arm around her then walked her inside. After he had calmed Keba down, he grabbed his glock and busted out.

YoungOne had made it home and took a hot shower. For some reason he couldn't get Jam and Power-Up off his mind. YoungOne put his Bluetooth in his ear and got his phone off the charger then dialed Power-Up's number and placed his phone back on the charger.

"What's up?" Power-Up answered.

"Bout fuckin time nigga. Me and A-K been trying to hit you and Jam all morning," YoungOne stated.

"I guess y'all didn't hear yet, huh?" Power-Up asked.

"Hear what?" YoungOne replied asking.

"Dude pulled his fuckin gun on me like I was a bitch ass nigga, bruh," Power-Up explained.

"Who the fuck you talking bout?" YoungOne asked and sensing he knew already who Power-Up was talking about.

"Jam violated, thug. And right now, my fuckin mind is playing tricks on me," Power-Up stated.

"Where all this shit coming from?" YoungOne asked but already knew the answer to his own question. He wanted to make sure he was right.

Dude think I'm fucking Keba," Power-Up said.

"Are you?" YoungOne asked.

"Come on YoungOne, I'm not weak, homie. He said she was off limits, so I'd never disrespect his mind," Power-Up responded.

"She left with you last night. What the hell dat was bout?" YoungOne asked.

Power-Up ran everything down to him bout taking Keba to the game and falling asleep at her house last night. After he finished running it, YoungOne asked, "And you didn't hit dat?"

"Nah, thug, I didn't. I wanted to, but I couldn't play Jam like dat," Power-Up answered.

"Well, what the fucking beef for?" YoungOne asked.

"Because he only going off of how he think what's going on with us," Power-Up replied.

"Where you headed now?" YoungOne inquired.

"Home," Power-Up stated.

"I'll be over there in bout an hour," YoungOne said.

"Aight," Power-Up said.

"You gonna call A-K, or you want me to?" YoungOne asked.

"You hit 'em up," Power-Up responded.

"Aight, one," YoungOne said.

"One," Power-Up responded back then hung up the phone.

Keba quickly took a shower and threw on her all white Coogi dress with her low top white Coogi tennis with no socks. When she finished dressing, she drove to the hospital to see Mini then headed over to her shop to clean up. She was cleaning up her office when she heard somebody knocking. She walked to the front thinking it was a customer even though she had the 'closed' sign still in the window. Keba looked straight into the eyes of Jam when she made it to the door. Being so disgusted at her brother, she just turned around to head back to her office to finish her cleaning. Jam started knocking harder like he was bout to break her window. That made her turn back around because she knew her brother could get crazy at times. Keba walked over to the door and opened it. She then stood there. Jam walked in past her. She locked the door back and continued what she was doing. But she knew that it was bout to be an argument.

"What I always told you bout niggaz like me?" Jam started.

"I'm not in the mood," Keba responded.

"What you wanna go through pain?" Jam asked.

"Just cause you take yo wife through pain, don't mean the next nigga gonna take me there," Keba shot back.

"You gotta a nigga dat treat you good," Jam replied.

"How the fuck you know dat?" Keba asked angrily pointing her finger.

"Don't make me kill my boy, Keba, because I will before I let him dog you," Jam stated, staring a hole through her.

"If you do, I promise you'll lose me as a sister," Keba said staring back.

"You stupid," Jam said shocking her with his statement.

"Get out!" Keba said in a loud voice.

"Do you love dude?" Jam asked.

"Yep," Keba answered in a matter-of-fact way.

"There's only one way y'all will be together, and that's if I'm dead," Jam stated then walked out Keba's shop.

As A-K was soaking in his hot tub, he nodded off for a few seconds. Hearing music playing, he quickly got out the tub knowing that if he stayed in it any longer he'd be stuck there for a while. He picked up his phone off the stand and answered it.

"What's up?" he asked.

"You talked to Jam yet?" YoungOne asked.

"Nah, that fool still not answering his shit," A-K replied.

"That shit he told you was bout Power-Up," YoungOne stated.

"You serious thug? What the fuck happened?" A-K asked sounding disappointed.

"Behind Keba," YoungOne responded.

"What he fuckin her?" AK asked.

Young One explained everything Power-Up told him about Jam accusing him of doing and bout pointing his gun at him.

"So what Power-Up did?" A-K asked YoungOne hoping nothing happened.

"He didn't say, but I think nothing," YoungOne replied.

"Man fuck, they trippin for real, where's Power-Up?" A-K asked.

"On his way home. I told him I'd be there in an hour," YoungOne responded.

"I'ma try and track Jam down. I'll get back atcha later. I'ma hit Power-Up, too," A-K stated.

"Aight, I'm on my way to holla at Power-Up," YoungOne said.

"Aight, one," A-K said.

"One," YoungOne replied back.

CHAPTER SIXTEEN

B oo woke up early and started his watch on Jam's wife. Just like always, she took her daughter to day care and drove her son to school then headed off to work. In a few days he would have 'em all hostage in their own home. After his survelliance on Tarnasha and her two kids, Boo drove by Keba's Beauty Salon to act like he wanted his hair hit up just to see what was going on. He'd only seen Keba's car there. Boo was happy she was alone. But, he had to make sure he didn't bump into Power-Up because that nigga might start being suspicious of him being round.

Boo got out his car, walked up to the door, and pulled it; but it was locked. Even though he'd seen the 'closed' sign on the door, Boo still wanted to make sure everything was gravy with him and Keba. So he began knocking anyway. He'd seen Keba walking from the back in a white Coogi dress. That dress should say "I'm all dat," he thought.

A-K put on his black and green LRG shirt, with the black LRG jeans, and some green and black Solja reebok.

A-K placed his 'Gutta Boy' chain on then grabbed his glock 40 and headed out the door. Once outside, A-K was trying to figure out which car he wanted to drive. After settling for the old-school money-green Cadillac with the all gold hundred spokes Dayton's, he hopped in the 'Lac and dialed Jam's number. He called Jam's number several times and didn't get an answer, so he went ahead and drove to Keba's Beauty Salon.

Jam drove to Clinton where he had a house stashed at for whenever he wanted to be alone. Sitting in the tub thinking about what to do about the situation with Power-Up and Keba made his head hurt just thinking about it. His phone kept ringing but he refused to answer it because he knew it was either YoungOne or A-K and he didn't feel like explaining why he pulled a gun on Power-Up. The only people he was going to answer for was his wife, or his mamma. Everybody else was on hold until he figured out what to do next. He was smoking on some Kush, and it had Jam's mind twisted. He was even thinking maybe he was down bad or maybe Power-Up was the one for Keba. But the lil man with the horns on his head kept him thinking evil. Jam got out the tub, dried off, and went laid across the king size sleep number. He adjusted the bed by remote to how he liked it and finished smoking his blunt 'til sleep invaded his world.

YoungOne threw on his red and white polo shirt, with some white Levi jeans, and a pair of red low top Converse. He put his red bandana around his neck, grabbed his glock-9, jumped in his candy apple red Escalade, and headed to Power-Up's house.

On the drive to Power Up's house, YoungOne passed by his baby LaShay's house for no apparent reason other than he wanted to see her. But like always, DJ 'nem was next door at their click house deep. When YoungOne passed by he could have sworn them niggaz put a mean mug on their faces as soon as he pulled up to the stop sign. Not being the messy type of dude, he kept on bout his business. He was just passing by the Chinese Store which made him realize he didn't have no cigars to roll his purp in. Since he was just passing through Prescott he stopped by the Yang Store in the area. A-K was a couple of blocks away from Keba's when he called Power-Up.

"What it do?" Power-Up asked when he answered the phone.

"Coolin, Thug on my way to Keba's," A-K responded.

"You talked to YoungOne?" Power-Up asked.

"Yeah, y'all trippin on some shit," A-K replied.

"He on some other shit," Power-Up said.

"So what it is?" A-K asked.

"I'm good, homie. Jam still my dude. I know he's going off his emotions right now, but I'ma get at him after he calms down," Power-Up stated.

"Do dat, because we fucking family, dude," A-K suggested.

"He just fuck me up by not trusting my loyalty, ya feel me," Power-Up replied.

"Well, I'm pulling up in front Keba's. I'ma try and catch up with Jam because he not answering the phone. I'ma get back atcha later," A-K said.

"Fa sho, one" Power-Up said.

"One," A-K replied back then hung up.

"What's up?" Boo was saying through the door once Keba made her way to it. Keba unlocked the door, seeing it was one of her new customers. She had to let him know that the shop would be open tomorrow.

""Hey, Boo. I won't be opening today," Keba said when she opened the door.

"I see that. What you re-arranging it around?" Boo asked

"No, actually, I was robbed last night so I'm just cleaning up," Keba responded.

"Damn, I' m sorry to hear that," Boo replied.

"It's cool. They wasn't nothing but a bunch of broke ass niggaz," Keba said with emotion. That last statement made Boo flinch. He had to catch himself from grabbing Keba and hitting her across the head with the 357 magnum under his shirt.

"I'ma let you get back to work. I'ma come by another time," Boo said turning around to leave.

"Alright, you do dat," Keba said closing the door to lock it until she saw A-K pulling up in the parking lot.

The Chinese store on Prescott kept a bunch of niggaz in front of it. YoungOne pulled up in front the store and almost got out the truck without his piece. He put his glock in front his jeans then made his way up to the Yang's Store. He purchased a box of cigars and couldn't leave without scoring a turkey wing. On his way out, YoungOne slowed up to see why the two niggaz was standing by his truck talking, but then they moved to where the rest of the niggaz was standing. Before walking out the store, YoungOne had eased his glock-9 from out his jeans and into his turkey wing bag.

"Say," one of the niggaz said soon as Young One stepped foot out the store.

"What's up?" YoungOne asked in reply looking in the direction from where the voice came.

"Dat bitch clean my nigga," the young looking dude said pointing at YoungOne's truck.

"Yeah, appreciate dat," YoungOne said then started back walking to his truck.

"Next time you come here in it, you won't leave with it," another nigga in the crowd said. Young One looked over at them and just shook his head. He got in his shit and cranked it up and headed to Power-Up's house.

A-K pulled on side the nigga with the dreads in his head and parked his car. He got out as dude was getting in his old school regal. A-K looked at the nigga and nodded his head in an upward motion speaking. For some reason, A-K was feeling like the nigga was acting nervous. But seeing Keba standing in the doorway, made him overlook dude's nervousness.

Boo had to get a hold of himself. Seeing A-K made his palms sweat. He wanted so badly to put that tool in dud's mouth and take his Cadillac. Boo started his car up and pulled out. Those fucking niggaz think they own Baton Rouge he thought to himself as he drove off. In a few days though, I'ma show 'em anybody can get it. He drove out the parking lot bobbing his head to his four six-by-nine across the back dash screaming dat Young Jeezy "Thug Motivation" CD.

A-K walked to the door where Keba was standing. "What's up?" he said giving her a hug.

"Chillin. Cleaning up this mess," Keba replied.

"Who that fool was dat just left?" A-K asked.

"A dude who just started coming here getting his dreads hit up," Keba answered.

"He must've thought I was yo man how nervous he was acting," A-K suggested walking by Keba to go inside the shop.

"Probably did," Keba said smiling then locking the door back.

"You talked to or seen Jam this morning?" A-K asked her.

"Uh huh. He came by here trippin this morning and talking some off the wall shit," Keba replied picking up stuff off the floor. A-K's mind went in a trance when Keba slightly bended over. His dick started rising because it seemed to have a brain of its own. He had to hurry up and shake back.

"Did he say where he was going?" A-K asked then started helping her pick up shit that was scattered over the floor.

"No, after we fussed he left, " Keba replied.

"I talked to Power-Up and he told me what happened. Jam just wants the best for you," A-K said looking at her.

"What you saying then is that Power-Up is not good enough for me?" Keba asked in a smart tone of voice.

"Nah, I'm not saying that at all. Jam just don't want none of his boys fuckin with his sister," A-K replied with a serious look on his face.

"Fuck that, what about me?" Keba said looking at A-K with tears in her eyes.

"You gotta understand, Keba," A-K said not knowing what to say to her after seeing the tears in her eyes.

"Well, he should understand too," Keba shot back. A-K was seeing a different side of Keba that had him wanting to go talk to Jam himself about her and Power-Up being together.

"I'll holla at Jam and see where his mind set at," A-K explained.

"My mind is already set," Keba said walking off in a soft but sexy walk.

A-K was bout to leave but seeing Keba sashay around cleaning her shop up and looking so delicious, he decided to stay and help her out since he didn't have nothing to do. His thoughts were going crazy watching Keba prance around in the dress that showed every curve she owned on her body. Even though he wouldn't ever disrespect his dawg Jam's mind by trying to get at Keba, he felt looking won't do no harm to anyone.

"I don't have shit to do so I can chill and help you clean up," A-K suggested.

"I'm good. But, if you wanna chill with me you can. I'll never stop a man from working," Keba said laughing.

For the rest of the day A-K and Keba cleaned up and talked shit about some of everything. Keba and A-K had made it to her office and started straightening things out when she realized her ring was missing out her desk drawer. She had placed it there the day before when she rushed home to go get ready to go to the game with Power-Up.

"Them bitches got my ring," Keba said looking at A-K.

"Who?" A-K asked with a confused look on his face.

"The niggaz who robbed my shop. Dat was my favorite ring too," Keba replied.

"Oh! The one with the 'K' in the middle surrounded by diamonds?" A-K asked.

"Uh huh, that's the one. I'll just get another one," Keba said and started back cleaning up. After they finished cleaning up, she wouldn't let A-K go unless he follow her to Darrlyn's Cafe where they sold all types of soul food. A-K agreed to let her buy him something to eat.

At Darrlyn's Cafe they ate a big meal then afterward hugged each other and went their separate ways.

YoungOne had made it to Power-Up's house. He and Power-Up was kickin it when Power-Up started telling YoungOne about how he feel bout Keba. He listened to everything Power-Up was running on how he got mad love for Keba and felt his pain because dat's how he had mad luv for LaShay. Even though he wouldn't dis his dawgs mind bout Keba, YoungOne understood how Power-Up felt because he was having the same feelings for girl. After they went thru the emotional stage, Power-Up grabbed the doja blunt and his cell phone. He lit up the blunt and made a call on his phone to the twins telling them to come over and that he had a treat for 'em looking at YoungOne.

"What the fuck dat mean?" YoungOne asked when he seen Power-Up looking at him talking bout a treat and smiling on the phone.

"Thug, the two twin hoes I been telling y'all bout. They said they wanna fuck the click," Power-Up said.

"Where them hoes at?" YoungOne then asked excitedly.

"They on their way over so let me bust you up on the pool table before they get here," Power-Up said standing up, stretching.

"Fuck, I forgot I told girl I was coming get her from school," YoungOne said out loud.

"Fuck it, you can catch those hoes another time" Power-Up suggested.

YoungOne quickly snatched his phone off his side and dialed LaShay's number.

"You wanna disturb a woman from getting her learn on, huh," LaShay said when she answered the phone.

"Nah, baby. I wanted to let you know I'ma be busy and I won't finish in time to pick you up from school," YoungOne replied feeling a lil guilty for lying to her.

"It's cool. I don't mind walking," she said in a playful tone.

"I'll make it up to you. And another thang, what kind of cars you like?" YoungOne asked.

"The kind you drive," LaShay shot back.

"To say you're seventeen years old, you show have a smart mouth," YoungOne said but at the same time loving every minute of it.

Call me later, boy, I gotta get back in class," LaShay said.

"Aight, lil mama. Be good," YoungOne replied.

"I will, and don't have me waiting on your call because it won't be nice if you do," LaShay said then hung up.

"It's good, Thug. Now let me bust ya ass on the pool table until them bad bitches come dat you brag bout," YoungOne said.

They were in their fifth game of pool when the door bell sounded off.

"There they go," Power-Up said, placed the pool stick on the rack, and then walked off to go answer the door. YoungOne started shooting all the pool balls in the pockets

thinking bout how he was about to fuck two twins, something he'd never done before.

"Hey there," one of the twins said when they entered
the pool room. He looked up from the shot he was bout
to take and almost lost his breath. The twins were standing there with different colored boy shorts with no top
on.

"Damn! Y'all some bad bitches," YoungOne replied
dropping the pool stick on the table. The twins started
moving in on YoungOne and before he knew it he was kissing two women at the same time.

"I'll be right back," Power-Up said then walked out the
room to go get his car keys so he could go hit a few blocks.
He knew the twins was bout to deal with YoungOne and
would be waiting on him next.

Two days after chillin with Keba, A-K had finally gotten
in touch with Jam. He and YoungOne's relationship with Jam
was still official. It had been three days since the robberies
and the Keba-Power-Up shit. Jam and Power-Up was still not
hollering at each other. A-K was getting aggravated for not
being able to kick it with all his boys at the same time. He was
cruising through Mayfair after leaving a lil hoe name Thalia
house. He picked up his phone to call YoungOne, and that's
when he spotted the same car that pulled up on side him and
shot his shit up. He placed the phone back down and hit the
block because now it was on.

All week everything was still the same and in two days it
all would go down. Boo had it all figured out and called his
clique up two days before letting them know it was time to
get real scrilla.

"This how it gotta happen," Boo said to his boys, "girl always passes by the Chicken Shack on her way home. She usually drives her black Benz. But lately, she's been driving her burgundy Lexus. Bouncy, you gonna go to the Chicken Shack and order some food to stay," Boo explained. He then took a sip of his drink before he continued to run down the plan. Bouncy was waiting on him to finish but Boo was taking his time.

"I want you to sit by the window where you can see the traffic. Me, Buck, and Seven gonna chill at the Pizza Hut a few blocks away from their house. Once you see the car you call me," Boo explained.

"What I'ma do then?" Bouncy asked.

"You ain't give me a chance to finish," Boo said passing a blunt to Buck.

"You gonna kill everybody in the Chicken Shack," Seven said bull-shittin and laughing.

"Fuck y'all," Bouncy replied.

"Man y'all chill and listen," Boo said getting his clique attention back on him.

"So it's gonna be her and two kids in the car?" Bouncy asked.

"Uh huh. It's gonna...nothing," Buck said about to crack a joke until he seen how Boo looked at him.

"This shit serious, while y'all playing," Boo said in an angry tone of voice.

"Fuck dat nigga and his boys," Seven said getting mad at Boo for acting so serious about the shit.

"I feel like dat too. But, I'm saying it's serious because we don't need no fucking neighbors seeing us, ya feel me?" Boo responded.

"Finish running it down," Bouncy said.

"When you call me, you get in yo car and come to the Pizza Hut. We'll be waiting on her to pass, so you just pull in and be cool. She has a car garage dat she most the times pull up in, but she work it by key. We gonna be in their neighborhood already. Bout time she start opening the garage, we gonna pull up behind her. Buck, you gonna drive while me and Seven gonna jump out and come up on each side of the car. There ain't too much traffic in their neighborhood. The shit should go smooth if it go down like this. Buck, you drive the car you'll be in to the Chicken Shack and leave it there. Seven gonna follow you in one of her cars to scoop you up then you two scoop Bouncy up because he gonna leave the car he in at Pizza Hut. Finally, y'all come back to the house so we all can be chillin waiting on that nigga Jam," Boo concluded to his crew.

"What if dude home already?" Bouncy asked.

"Lately he been chillin at home, but he always leave before his wife and kids make it back," Boo responded.

"Well, let's do the damn thang," Buck replied anxiously.

Boo then stuck his hand out and the rest of 'em did the same, "on a count of three," Boo said. "One, two, three!"

"The Hitting Licks Clique!" they all shouted at once.

For the past week Power-Up had been laying up with Meka and Mecko just fuckin. Keba had been calling everyday asking him to go out to eat or come chill at her place but he'd been refusing. It took everything in him to be turning her down like dat. Power-Up had been trying to call Jam several times during the week, but his calls kept being transferred to the automatic voice mail each time. Many times, Power-Up was tempted to drive out to Jam's house but he didn't wanna start no bull shit. He felt like he needed some air, so he got up out the bed put on his Gucci outfit and left out the door headed for the Sports Bar.

After picking up his baby from school, YoungOne not being no dumb nigga, was chillin at LaShay's house helping her study for a test at school for the next day.

"Let's take a break," LaShay said.

"Wanna walk to the store?" YoungOne asked.

"I don't care," LaShay replied.

They made it outside and were on their way to the Yang Store when one of the niggaz next door hollered out.

"Dude, you a long way from home," the nigga spoke.

Being that he was with LaShay, YoungOne played it off like he didn't even hear it. YoungOne and LaShay had made it to the store. They brought some ice cream and other lil snacks for themselves and were on the way back to her house. YoungOne noticed DJ and four of his boys was coming their way. He placed his arm around LaShay neck hugging her to make DJ nem mad. He and LaShay was walking on the right side of the street while DJ nem was walking in the middle. But once they became closer, DJ and his boys all proceeded on the right side of the street. At dat moment, YoungOne knew it was bout to turn out bad. On the strength of LaShay he had been sparring these clowns. But this time, YoungOne felt they was testing his manhood. DJ and his boys all formed a straight line one behind the other and when they came close enough to him the first dude in line bumped YoungOne. Before the second one got a chance to do the same, YoungOne dropped the bag he was holding and punched him square in the face. Dude stumbled backward trying to recuperate. The other four niggaz bum rushed YoungOne and was dealing with him when LaShay hit one of the dudes trying to help her man. The first nigga YoungOne hit had shook back from the blow and slapped spit out LaShay's mouth. YoungOne had lost his balance and was on the ground getting stumped. He got up with his glock-40 and shot all five of the niggaz. Someone saw him getting crowded and called the police. LaShay was crying hysterically because of how one of the niggaz was laying right by her feet with a bullet in his head. YoungOne picked the bag and phone up off the ground then grabbed LaShay's hand and walked off.

People started rushing toward DJ nem trying to help them survive. YoungOne and LaShay had made it about fifty feet away from the shooting when police cars started pulling up to the scene. YoungOne looked back and saw a few of the police scrambling to their cars looking his way. He knew right then and there somebody had pointed him out. He heard the engines of the police cars coming his way so he dialed A-K's number.

"Tell my brother what happened," YoungOne said handing LaShay the phone as soon as one of the police cars pulled in front them and two more stopping behind them.

A-K reached under the seat and retrieved his other glock then placed it on his lap where the other one was laying. He was parked across the street in the apartment complex waiting because no matter who got in that car he was napping them. A-K started thinking bout going knocking on the front door when his phone sounded off playing dat Boosie, which brought him out his zone. A-K was contemplating on sending YoungOne straight to the voice mail but knowing he wouldn't hear the end of it, he placed the phone to his ear. "What's up?" A-K answered.

Power-Up had made it inside the Sports Bar and spotted the lil hoe Sugar Doo that Jam be fuckin and dat he himself wanted to fuck. She was standing by the poker machines playing one of them.

"Hey sexy," Power-Up greeted easing up on girl.

"I've been waiting on you to come here alone," she said when she turned around and seen him.

"Well, you don't have to wait no more," Power-Up stated smiling at her.

"Everytime I think of you my pussy get wet," Sugar Doo said.

"So you telling me that pussy wet right now?" Power-Up asked her.

"Soak and wet," she responded then walked off to the ladies room twisting. Once she made it to the bathroom door Sugar Doo grabbed her pussy like a man grabs his dick through her Dereon jeans and beckoned for Power-Up to come to the bathroom.

Power-Up didn't need any more invitations the way he speeded off walking to where Sugar Doo had disappeared inside the ladies room. He made it to the bathroom door and stopped to check his pockets for a condom. After feeling one in his pocket he walked in the bathroom to find Sugar Doo in one of the stalls naked putting her six inch heels back on. When she placed her heels back o,n she then pulled Power-Up all the way in the small-spaced stall then dropped to her knees to suck the skin off his dick.

Jam had kind of shook back from the little drama he and Power-Up was going through. It was two days before he and his dawgs were supposed to go on his last re-up. He was cruising through the streets of Baton Rouge thinking about whether he should let Power-Up and Keba do them. After all, dats my dude and it'd be better to be him than a fake ass nigga. Jam was thinking that when he made a left turn on Eaton Street heading toward Charles Street.

Hearing police sirens through the phone had A-K all fucked up because he knew something happened. LaShay was trying to explain to him on the phone but he heard in the background, "Put y'all hands up!"

"Who this and where YoungOne at?" A-K asked. LaShay explained to him what had just happened. YoungOne was being handcuffed, and now the police were walking toward her like they wanted to shoot her.

"Look call me back in a few minutes if they don't take you in for questioning," A-K stated.

"Aight," LaShay said then hung up.

Fuck! A-K said to himself and for his brother YoungOne and because he had to leave without finding out who was the driver of the Delta-88. He pulled out the apartment complex calling Jam's phone at the same time.

Jam made it to the corner of Eaton Street and Charles Street and was stopped by a street full of people crying, hugging each other, and whispering like something bad had happened even though he saw lines of police cars deeper in the curb. He was about to roll down his window to ask somebody standing around what happened until his phone started vibrating.

"What's up, Thug?" Jam answered seeing it was A-K's number.

"Girl just called me who YoungOne just started kicking it with, saying he shot five niggaz a few minutes ago," A-K said soon as he heard Jam voice.

"You talking bout girl out the curb, huh?" Jam asked to make sure.

"Yeah, that's her," A-K replied.

"Man, I'm over in that area now. I see the streets packed with police cars and people," Jam responded. A-K was bout to mention seeing the car the niggaz was driving who shot his car up but held back until the situation with YoungOne got handled.

"Where you headed?" A-K asked.

"Meet me at the Sports Bar. I'ma send the lawyer to see what's up," Jam stated.

"I'll see you when you make it to the Sports Bar. One," A-K responded.

"One, and call Power-Up and have him come, too," Jam said then hung up.

Even though girl head game was nice, Power-Up had other thangs on his mind like busting that pussy up. He pulled the rubber out his pocket, took his dick outa SugarDoo mouth. When she seen him take the plastic off the rubber she stood on her feet and snatched the rubber out his hand and placed it on his dick quickly. Power-Up started sucking on her titties one at a time. Her pussy was on fire by the way she was stroking his dick and she wanted so badly to feel it in her. SugarDoo raised one leg on the toliet and stuck Power-Up manhood in her womanhood. They was going stroke for stroke when Power-Up phone started playing that

Lil Boosie 'Touchdown To Cause Hell.' Looking down at the number Power-Up picked it up to answer only because it was his dawg calling.

"Bad timing," Power-Up said when he answered.

"Don't tell me you fucking something nigga," A-K stated.

"Then I won't tell you then, but you got me right," Power-Up said.

"Dat shit gotta hold on my nigga. YoungOne caught up in some shit," A-K said.

"What?" Power-Up asked but continued slow stroking girl at the same time. A-K went on to explain what LaShay said about the incident. Hearing that Power-Up had finally pulled his dick outta girl pussy and took the rubber off.

"Where they took him to?" Power-Up then asked.

"I think the precinct on Plank Road. But, I talked to Jam and he wants us to meet him at the Sports Bar," A-K stated.

"I'm already here at the Sports Bar," Power-Up said.

"I thought you was. . . never mind. I'll holla when I get there," A-K replied.

"Aight, one," Power-Up said.

"One," A-K returned then hung up.

Power-Up had lost all interest in SugarDoo after hearing bout YoungOne.

"We'll, we have to finish this another time," Power-Up said to Sugar Doo putting his dick back in his pants and walking out the bathroom.

All day Keba had been having bad feelings like something bad was going to happen. But being that she never received any phone calls giving her bad news, she over looked her gut feelings. No sooner than Keba finished doing a lady's hair in a Mohawk, she dialed her brother's number. They haven't talked since he came by her shop with the bullshit.

"Hey, baby sis," Jam answered on the other end. Keba was surprised to hear those words because from her knowledge Jam and Power-Up still wasn't talking.

"Hey, big bro," Keba said back. Then the phone went silent.

"What's on ya mind lil sis?" Jam asked sensing Keba's sadness.

"Nothing, just wanted to know how you doing," she replied.

"I'm good," Jam responded.

"You sure?" she asked.

"Yeah, I'm sure. Now, where you at?" Jam asked.

"I'm at the shop," Keba answered.

"Come to the Sports Bar," Jam said.

"Right now?" Keba asked.

"Uh, huh. YoungOne just shot some niggaz on Charles Street and me and A-K are on our way to the Sports Bar until the lawyers contact me and let us know what's up, so come chill with me," Jam suggested.

"Alright, I'm on my way," Keba said.

"Love ya, and see ya when you make it," Jam said.

"Love you, too," Keba said back then hung up. Keba told the women in the shop what happened then walked outside. She jumped in her Camry then it hit her—what her brother said about him and A-K meeting up, but he never mentioned Power-Up. She was bout to call Power-Up and let him know to meet them at the Sports Bar but changed her mind because she wasn't in no mood to see the two people she loved go at it. So instead, she just drove the way there in silence.

A-K pulled in the parking lot of the Sports Bar thinking about Young One but at the same time his mind on also seeing that Delta-88. Fuck that, I'ma bust a bitch head tonight he mumbled to himself before turning his car off and getting out with his forty-five. He headed inside where Power-Up was. A-K made it to where Power-Up was sitting at a table getting his sip on.

"What it do?" Power-Up asked reaching his hand out giving A-K pound.

"You know I'm fuck up right now," A-K responded giving Power-Up pound back.

"What the fuck happened?" Power-Up asked.

"Girl couldn't really run it down to me, but she said it was a fight," A-K said.

"Bitch ass niggaz probably jumped YoungOne," Power-Up suggested. As soon as he finished his sentence and looked up, he and Jam caught eyes as Jam was walking toward the table. Seeing the look in Power-Up's eyes, A-K turned around to see what he was looking at.

"What's up?" Jam said giving A-K and Power-Up dap.

"You found out anything?" A-K asked Jam.

"I hollered at a few people who was standing out there and they said the niggaz crowded YoungOne. He fell down and they started stumping him, then they heard gun shots being fired," Jam explained.

"What, it happened at her house?" A-K asked.

"Nah, they had walked to the Yang Store," Jam replied.

"YoungOne said he felt it was gonna be some shit outta them niggaz," Power-Up said.

"I sent the lawyers to find out what precinct he's at and what the charges are," Jam said.

Keba pulled in the parking lot and seen a lime green Charger with the top cut off that looked nice. But, what caught her eyes was the all yellow Dodge Magnum sitting on 24s and only one person in Baton Rouge owned that color. She was wondering what Power-Up was doing there. She hurried up and made it inside to see what was going on.

Looking around soon as she entered through the door Jam spotted her and raised his hands up. She saw Power-Up sitting at the table, and it slowed her heart rate down knowing everything was all good.

"Hey y'all," Keba said when she reached the table then started giving her brother 'nem hugs. Jam went on and told his sister what happened with YoungOne. After updating Keba, Jam started apologizing to her and Power-Up for the way he handled the situation with them. Once everybody calmed down, A-K told 'em how he ran across the Delta-88 in Mayfair and what he was bout to do when YoungOne's girl called him telling him about the shooting.

"Why the hell you ain't called none of us?" Power-Up asked looking at A-K stupidly.

"I didn't have time," A-K replied.

"How the fuck you didn't nigga?" Jam asked also looking at A-K fucked-up.

"Well, I'ma take care them fools tonight," A-K stated.

"We going withcha, fuck wrong with you," Jam replied.

"Nah, I'ma go. You stay back and handle business with YoungOne," Power-Up said to Jam.

Even though she knew they was talking about killing somebody, Keba was just happy to see her brother nem back straight, so she just sat back and enjoyed the moment.

Word passed fast about the shooting. Boo was making a crack sell when the junkie told him a nigga name YoungOne shot some niggaz out the curb. Being that he wasn't that far away from where it happened, he walked to Charles Street and found out more details. Knowing DJ nem was doing it big and bout dat mess made Boo kind of angry because now he had no time to waste on robbing Jam. It's bout to be a fuckin war he said to himself as he headed back to Prescott.

It'd been three hours since the shooting and they still hadn't heard nothing. Then Jam's phone started vibrating.

"What's good?" Jam answered a little tipsy. The lawyer told him YoungOne was taken to the parish prison about five minutes ago and charged with 5 counts of attempted murder.

"What's up with the bond?" Jam asked. Power-Up, Keba, and A-K put all their attention on Jam because they knew it had to be the lawyer for YoungOne. The lawyer told him that YoungOne might not get a bond until in the morning.

"You need to get him one soon and call me back," Jam said in the phone then hung up. He related what the lawyer said to his boys and sister.

"How much you think the bond gonna hit for?" Keba asked.

"About two-hundred grand," Power-Up answered.

"It really don't matter," Jam said for no reason and taking a sip outta his Henney and coke.

"Man, shit been quiet bout them robberies. Whoever that was ain't running their mouths," Power-Up said out loud.

"I even been checking out pawn shops to see if some-body pawned my ring," Keba said also out loud.

"The one I brought with the 'K' circled in diamonds?" Jam asked.

"Uh, huh. That was my favorite ring," Keba replied.

"Power-Up gonna replace it for you," Jam stated. Everybody at the table looked up at Jam all thinking the same thing. This nigga going to be trippin again until Jam said, "You got her, huh dude?" looking at Power-Up smiling.

"Like a dog," Power-Up replied. Jam got up out his seat and beckoned for everybody to follow him. The rest of the night they shot partners pool: Power-Up and A-K against Jam and Keba. After Power-Up and A-K tied it up at four games apiece, they went back to their table to talk business. "Y'all know tomorrow we take that ride so A-K you gonna have to put that on hold until we get back," Jam said.

"Man, me and Power-Up can handle that and be ready to roll tomorrow," A-K suggested.

"You know this my last go round and shit need to go down as planned," Jam replied.

"Shit gonna go as planned. It won't take all night," A-K said.

"Just be ready at 6:00 in the morning. If YoungOne don't make bond by that time, we'll see him when we get back," Jam stated.

"Aight, dats a bet," A-K said.

"It's getting dark so we can go start on that piece of busi-ness," Power-Up said looking at A-K.

"Look, when y'all finish come out to my house in Zachary," Jam said then stood up to leave.

"Fa show," Power-Up said giving Jam dap then hugged Keba. A-K followed in pursuit and dapped Jam and hugged Keba, too. They were walking out when Sugar Doo popped out of nowhere walking up on Jam.

"YoungOne should call you once he hit central booking. Tell dat fool one luv and don't drop the soap," Power-Up said as him and A-K busted out to go body a nigga or a few. Jam bull shitted with girl for a few minutes then he and Keba busted out their separate ways.

Power-Up and A-K had driven out to A-K's house to change clothes into all black. When they were dressed, A-K then hopped in the car with Power-Up and they drove downtown to the Belle of Baton Rouge Casino so A-K could steal a car. He snatched a blue F-150 out the parking lot. Power-Up followed him to his lil bitch house in Mayfair. Power-Up left his car in girl yard then jumped in the truck with A-K carrying the choppa on deck with him. A-K called girl to let her know he'd be over later on and that he was in the car that was in her yard. As they were getting closer Power-Up made sure the silencer was on his Glock-40 straight, and the one on A-K's forty-five good. They pulled in the apartment complex and waited for the Delta 88 to show up.

YoungOne had finally got a chance to make a phone call.

"Hello," Jam answered the phone seeing a strange number that said pay phone.

Hearing the operator say collect call, Jam pressed zero before the operator finished.

"What's up, thug?" Jam asked. "I'm good," YoungOne responded. "What's up with the bond?" Jam asked.

"These bitches talking bout I have to wait 'til in the morning," YoungOne replied.

"I was at the Sports Bar earlier with A-K and Power-Up and he found the car dat hit him up so him and Power-Up 'red rum,'"Jam stated.

"Gutta Boyz back together again?" YoungOne asked.

"Like shit never happen," Jam answered.

"That's what's up," YoungOne replied.

"We taking dat ride in the morning, ya feel me? If you don't make out in time, lay low until we get back," Jam explained.

"Aight," YoungOne said.

"Oh yeah, Power-Up said one luv and don't drop the soap," Jam said laughing.

"Tell that nigga fuck him," YoungOne replied laughing back. A recorded monitor come on the phone letting them know they had sixty seconds left on the call.

"Call me back," Jam said.

"I'ma hit my baby up, too, and see how she doing. They only gave me two calls," YoungOne said.

"Well, Keba gonna have everything when you get a bond if we gone," Jam explained.

"Fa show, one," YoungOne said.

"One," Jam said back then the phone went dead.

Boo had his clique in his apartment getting ready for the next day. He started telling them bout the shit happened with YoungOne. Some of 'em had heard what went down from the streets. Boo let them know tomorrow it had to go down because the Gutta Boyz was bout to be in some serious beef. "We must get us before this shit pop off," Boo said passing the purp blunt to the next man.

"You think dat fool gonna give it up?" Buck asked.

"He won't have a choice," Seven said raising the chopa up off the floor.

"I think this. I don't believe he got nothing at his crib where he lay his head, but he can take us to it," Boo explained.

"You talking big thangs, right?" Bouncy asked.

"Something to put us all the way in the game where we gonna be the man," Boo replied.

"Let's get it," Seven said blowing Buck a charge off the blunt.

"We almost there," Boo said looking at his boys. They called some hoes over to finish the night and smoked blunt after blunt plus drunk big cups of syrup off the lick from the barber shop. They all talked shit to each other until one by one they all eased off to a room with one of the females. Even if it was the kitchen floor where one of them had a bitch legs wide open eating her pussy, they still felt on top.

Power-Up and A-K decided to wait in the yard where the Delta-88 was parked. They eased out the F-150 with Power-Up placing his forty-five on his side grabbed the choppa and headed across the street with A-K right behind him with his 45' tucked in his pants. They were sitting behind a parked car that looked like it had been sitting up for years.

Power-Up and A-K were sitting there in silence when they heard loud music and a nigga trunk rattling, but it sounded a few blocks away. A-K took his ski mask off and spit then the head lights blinded him. He hurried and put his ski mask back on and grabbed his 45'. But it wasn't the Delta-88. A Honda Accord pulled in and a female in a pair of skinny jeans stepped out talking on the cell phone. A-K wanted to ambush girl and take her inside until whoever driving the Delta showed up. But, Power-Up insisted they wait on the car. As soon as girl made it inside, A-K military-style, crawled to one of the back windows of the house and started trying to see inside. He found the room window girl was in and watched her talk on the phone as she took off her clothes at the same time. The chick had an ass so fat dat A-K considered on coming back and finding girl after he spanked whoever dude was to her. He was so stalked out that he damn near forgot he was on a mission until Power-Up crept up on him.

"What the fuck you doing," Power-Up asked whispering. A-K was startled when he heard Power-Up's voice.

"Thug, this hoe finer than a mutha fucka," A-K said grabbing his dick. Power-Up looked through the window and saw what A-K was talking bout. Girl was lying across the bed on her back with both her legs up in a pair of orange lace panties and an orange top.

"Damn bitch is fine. But, we ain't here to stalk. Let's roll," Power-Up said looking at A-K then walked off. They made it back in position where the choppa was and a few minutes later the Delta pulled in. The nigga fumbled around in the car for a few seconds then made his way out. Soon as he stepped foot on solid ground, A-K and Power-Up was in his face. Seeing Power-Up holding the choppa a few inches from his head dude started panicking.

"This all I got," dude said bout to go in his pocket.

"This ain't no fucking stick up nigga," A-K stated. Hearing that really had dude confused. A-K took off his mask and asked dude who shot up his car with an evil look in his eyes. Dude started stuttering but before he could say anything, A-K let off three shots to the head out his 45'. Dude fell, and Power-Up handed A-K the choppa who hit dude six more times with his 40. They hauled ass to the stolen F-150.

After the moments spent with her brother nem even though it was a bad time, Keba was feeling good because they was back as the Gutta Boyz. She had made her way back to her beauty salon and talked shit with her girls about the dog ass niggaz. Keba drove home and fixed herself a hot bubble bath with some epson salt in it. She was lying back relaxing her body and mind. Before Keba knew it she was massaging her clitoris thinking bout how sexy Power-Up was looking today. Almost at the point of exploding her phone started ringing. She was feeling like if YoungOne had not been in jail, that call would have to wait. Getting up out the tub to get her phone off the stand, she seen dude number she so-called fuck with, and it made her want to break her $150 phone. Letting it ring, Keba laid back in the tub and nodded off.

Jam had called up the two white girls and had them to come to his crib to be ready for the ride. Driving to Texas to pick up supply had always been dangerous, but for the past few years. Jam started fucking one of the pill headed ass white girls, and since then shit been a whole lot easier. It was only a ten percent chance that the police would stop some innocent little white girls. All he had to do was drive out there, get it and transfer it to where the snow bunnies would be waiting at the hotel. Jam kept them supplied with all types of pills and some black dick and they were satisfied. He was lying across the bed with the two white girls when he heard a hard knock. Off top he knew it was Power-Up and A-K.

"Hold Up," Jam hollered walking to the door. He peeped through the curtain to make sure it was them. When he'd seen A-K, Jam unlocked the door and walked off.

"YoungOne called?" A-K asked.

"Yeah," Jam answered.

"What he say?" A-K asked really missing his dawg.

"He's good. Said they gonna give him a bond in the morning," Jam replied.

Power-Up had made it inside after sitting in the car talking to the twins who wanted him to come knock their boots. Power-Up locked the door and walked in the room where Jam and A-K was.

"What's up?" Power-Up asked.

"Shit. YoungOne said fuck you," Jam related. Power-Up was standing in the door way when the white girls walked in the room with long night shirts on.

"Hey, guys," they said in unison climbing in the bed with Jam.

"We sharing?" A-K asked out loud to no one but looking at the white girls.

"Chill, nigga. We need our rest for in the morning," Jam stated looking at A-K. A-K went from happy to mad instantly.

"You don't have to be jealous, I'm not fuckin either," Power-Up said looking at A-K.

"Fool, I'm not jealous, I just wanted to smash some pussy," A-K said looking at Jam.

"Then you gonna get full of them pills and ain't gonna quit," Jam said grabbing his mojo joint.

"I'm already full of them," A-K stated.

"Thug, you fucked up I'm going to sleep. Just be ready at 5:00 in the morning," Jam said then climbed under the satin sheets still puffing on his joint.

"I'll see y'all at five," Power-Up said walking off to go take a shower then get some Zzzzzs. A-K looked at the white girls with pure lust in his eyes because he felt like Jam gave him the green light long as they be ready when the time arrived. The white girls kissed Jam on the jaw and followed A-K to a different room to go get dicked down.

Boo couldn't sleep. His mind kept wandering off to how good he needed shit to go. He got out the bed leaving the sexy freak sound asleep. Boo grabbed one of the rolled blunts off the table on his way to stand outside on the balcony. He looked in the sky and almost said a silent prayer. But, he changed his mind not wanting to ask god to help him do evil. He smoked half of the blunt then headed back inside to try again to get some sleep.

"Bitch ass nigga I told you I was gonna get it one way or the other. Now look at you, can't do shit with ya hands and feet tied up. Ya feel helpless huh? I know nigga. You never expected me huh? Look atcha boys tied up in dat cell. I ordered them to violate ya manhood. Nobody would hear y'all. Everybody at chow."

"Man get up. It's time to roll. You musta been dreaming because all you kept saying was 'fuck you'," Jam said.

"Thug, I was dreaming a nigga had us tied up then the dream switched like we was in prison," Power-Up replied eyes bucked wide open and heart beating fast.

"You outcha top, I'ma go wake A-K and them lil freaks up," Jam said walking off. Power-Up remained lying down for a few more minutes trying to replay the dream he was having.

"You up, huh Power-Up?" Jam hollered from another room.

"Yeah," Power-Up answered.

Jam got himself situated and made sure everyone else was doing the same. Then he went outside and warmed both of the vehicles up to hit the highway.

Sleep had finally invaded his world. Boo felt like soon as he closed his eyes the alarm clock was sounding off letting him know it was 5:45 in the morning. He took a hot shower, got dressed and found the blunt he was smoking last night then went jumped in his whip.

Puffing on his blunt, Boo slowed his car down to a halt and looked closely at the brick house as it was coming to life by the way lights in different rooms was on. It was after six o'clock so he knew soon Jam's wife would be making her way to do her daily routine. Boo drove off thinking about how he was bout to change the game.

Before hitting the highway Jam 'nem stopped at the Waffle House and ate a big breakfast. Rolling down I-10 highway, Jam called Keba to let her know the lawyer was gonna contact her.

"Man, you was talking bout I wouldn't gonna stop. Those fucking white girls out their fuckin minds," A-K said from the back seat.

"I know, dats why I didn't want you to start those hoes," Jam stated.

"They look like they don't get enough," Power-Up said leaning back in the passenger seat.

"Man, the short one wanted to eat my ass," A-K said laughing.

Power-Up and Jam was laughing so hard they had tears coming out their eyes. "I let them bitches eat mine," Jam said. That had all three of em laughing.

"You a fuckin freak, nigga," Power-Up stated.

"Dat shit feel good, thug," Jam replied.

"Fuck dat. Bitch ain't playing round my ass," A-K said.

"They not gonna stick nothing in ya ass fool," Jam put in.

"Just the thought of a nigga ass," Power-Up said still laughing.

"You know who put me on that shit, Power-Up?" Jam asked.

"Who?" Power-Up asked back.

"Dat boy Young Muzzy out the Bottom," Jam answered.

"You talking bout 'B' that was on lock with us?" Power-Up asked to make sure they was on the same page.

"Uh, huh," Jam replied. They were half way to Texas when Jam told Power-Up to call the white girls who were trailing behind them to let em know that they were bout to pull over at the next gas station.

Laying down on a flat mattress with no sheets in Central booking, YoungOne was called out the cell to go in front the t.v. screen to see the judge. The Judge read out his charges then set his bond at four-hundred and seventy-five-thousand-dollars. YoungOne's lawyer contacted Keba and told her what was up. YoungOne was back in the holding cell pacing the floor, which smelled like urine. Thirty minutes later, the deputy called his name to let him know that his bond had been posted.

It was getting closer to that time and the shit had Boo anxious. He ran how it was gonna go down to his clique one more time. Everyone was ready. All Boo had to do was say the word, and they would all be in their positions. The way Boo put it, they was bout to ball like Jordan.

Keba was sitting in the Parish Jail waiting on YoungOne to come out. She turned her radio up a little then leaned her seat back and let Keysha Cole blare through the speakers. Keba didn't see YoungOne walking up on the car until he knocked on the door window bringing her out her daze. When she saw that it was YoungOne, Keba started smiling turning her radio down. Then, she hit the switch to unlock the door. She got out the car and hugged YoungOne. He walked around to the passanger side and climbed in. Keba made her way back in the car after taking a few moments to look out at the prison. Keba started her XL-Yukon up and pulled out into the morning light.

"Jam said for you to lay back until they make it back," Keba said.

"I know, he told me that when I called him last night," YoungOne replied.

"You got this weird ass smell on you," Keba stated holding her nose letting the windows down then back up.

"I know. It smells like nothing but piss in them cells," YoungOne said sniffing himself.

"Anything you need for me to do?" Keba asked.

"Nah, you can take me home. I gotta hit the shower," YoungOne responded.

"That's fa sure," Keba said frowning up at him.

"I gotta see my baby," YoungOne said.

"Just be careful. I also need to meet this young lady I hear you crazy bout," Keba suggested pulling up in front YoungOne crib.

"Thank you," YoungOne said before reaching over giving Keba a hug. He opened the door and climbed out.

Jam nem made it to the Exxon gas station, filled the cars with gas, brought some stuff to snack on, and then hit the highway once again. Jam's phone started playing Trick Daddy's 'Thug Holiday'. He knew then that it was Young One calling.

"What's up, Thug?" Jam answered.

"Coolin," YoungOne said.

"Everything good?" Jam asked.

"Long as I'm out dat hell hole, I'm good," YoungOne stated.

"I feel dat," Jam said.

"Tell dat fool, what's up?" A-K said to Jam.

"A-K holla," Jam related through the phone then "much luv" he related back to A-K.

"Tell dat nigga I said 'one,'" Power-Up said.

"Same thang," Jam said back to Power-Up. He hung the phone up with YoungOne then he drove the rest of the way to Texas.

CHAPTER SEVENTEEN

YoungOne wanted to surprise LaShay about being home so instead of using the cell phone he decided to use his house phone because he never gave her that number.

Ring, Ring!

"Hello," her sweet voice answered.

"I miss you," YoungOne confessed.

"Who is this?" LaShay asked.

"I ain't been locked down dat long for you to forget my voice," YoungOne said.

"Hey baby, where you at?" LaShay asked.

"I just made it home," YoungOne responded.

"It's been crazy round here," LaShay stated.

"I been trying to avoid those clowns as much as I could but they went too far," YoungOne answered.

"I know. They asked for that," LaShay replied.

"I'ma come get you from school," YoungOne said.

"I'm at home," she said.

"Why you didn't go to school?" YoungOne asked.

"My mama said it was best if I stay out of sight for a few days," LaShay responed.

"I wanna come see you," YoungOne suggested.

"That's not a good idea," LaShay stated.

YoungOne and LaShay talked on the phone until late into the evening. After they finished talking, YoungOne felt he needed some air and decided he would go to the strip club. He figured he'd go to the one that Power-Up goes to all the time. Plus, he wished the twins were there.

Boo kept telling his clique that the time had arrived and they needed to keep their heads focused because they didn't need any mistakes. It was getting dark earlier this time of year, so he felt that played in their favor. Boo had everyone already in position. The only thing they were waiting on was for Jam's wife and kids to make their way home.

Eating that pizza had Buck's stomach hurting like hell. As soon as he made it to the bathroom, Boo's phone started ringing. He looked at Seven then at his phone shaking his head because it was Bouncy calling.

"She on her way?" Boo asked soon as he put the phone to his ear.

"Nah, that's why I'm calling to ask you what's up?" Bouncy replied.

"Man, you fucking trippin. Be cool. Bitch coming home," Boo stated angrily.

"There she go right there!" Bouncy said through the phone in a loud voice.

"You know what to do," Boo said then hung the phone up

"Where the hell is Buck?" Boo asked looking around.

"In the bathroom," Seven answered.

"Man, go get dat fool. I'm going get in the car," Boo said walking quickly out of Pizza Hut.

They had finally made it to Dallas, Texas. Jam sent the white girls to the hotel with A-K while he and Power-Up went copped the bricks and pills. Jam was the type to never let the connect know when he was leaving. He would always give 'em a wrong day on when he'd be hitting the highway. And today he decided to score and come right back by taking a different route. He called A-K and told him to bring the car to his uncle's crib, who did not live too far away from the room. After putting the bricks of coke and pills in the car for the white girls to drive back, A-K brought the car back. They all were back on the highway trying to make it back safely in the same manner they arrived.

YoungOne entered the strip club and damn near passed out seeing all the bad bitches inside. Even though he'd seen and fucked a lot of nice women, he understood why Power-Up stayed in this strip club. He brought himself a drink then headed straight to the stage to see some ass shaking.

Boo made it to the rock renter and jumped in the driver seat because if Buck was not ready they were going to leave him.

"Fuck," he ranted, hitting the steering wheel realizing Buck had the fuckin keys. Boo was swearing on a stack of bibles that if Buck make them miss girl passing he was gonna kill him, but his mindset was instantly changed when he saw Buck and Seven jogging to the car. Boo climbed over to the passanger seat as Buck hopped in the driver seat and Seven jumped in the back. Buck started the car and no later than twenty seconds had passed when Jam's wife stopped at the red light.

"There she go," Boo said.

The light turned green then Buck pulled out behind her. Right before Boo and his clique set up their post, he passed by Jam's house a few times to make sure he wasn't there.

Since Jam owned several whips, Boo still didn't know for sure if he was home. Buck slowed down a little to let Jam's wife get ahead but not that far.

"Turn right here," Boo said. He had come up with an idea earlier that morning. Instead of following girl, they would go the opposite way and get head on with her when she turned on the street where her house was.

Jam hadn't seen his wife and kids in two days. He knew his wife figured he wouldn't be back until the next day. He was feeling like he had a free night to hit the club since he hadn't been in a long time. But, missing her made him call to let her know he'd be home later on that night.

Ring, Ring, Ring!

"Hey honey," she answered.

"Hey baby, what's up?" Jam replied asking.

"I'm good. I'm on my way home," she responded.

"Where my babies?" Jam asked.

"Ty sitting in the back seat playing on his iPad, and you know Tyesha sitting up here in the front seat asleep like always," she stated.

"I'll be home later on tonight," Jam replied.

"You not staying out there?" his wife asked.

"Nah, I need some dessert," Jam replied laughing.

"Well, it sure will be waiting on you to do whatever you like," she responded.

"Well, I'll see you tonight and tell my babies I love them," Jam said.

"Alright. Love you baby," she responded

"Love you more," Jam said then hung up.

YoungOne was sitting at the stage watching a stripper in a pink thong with Juicy tattooed across her ass. Off top this stripper made him forget about the twins. He pulled out a stack of money from his pocket and started throwing hundreds and fifties at Juicy. Seeing the 'Gutta Boy' chain on YoungOne's neck she knew he was one of Power-Up's boys and that he had money. She moved closer to YoungOne and started making her ass clap then she laid on her back and spread her legs open grinding while making sex faces. YoungOne stuck three hundred dollars in her thong, but Juicy wasn't finished yet. She grabbed one of her titties and started sucking it looking YoungOne in the eyes. All the other niggaz at the stage got mad because of how she was giving YoungOne all the attention.

Juicy climbed up on one of the poles and started acting and doing her thing. When she finished, YoungOne had enough, so he got up and went to the VIP section. She found out where he went and made her way up there with a bottle of Moet with the intention of introducing herself to another Gutta Boy.

Being the wife to one of Baton Rouge most established drug dealer kept Tarnasha alert at all times even when a muthafucka thought otherwise. She spotted the red Maxima when it pulled out the Pizza Hut behind her after the light turned green. Not really expecting anything, she paid the three dudes no mind, but now pulling up in her drive way and seeing the same car a few feet away gave her a bad feeling that something terrible was about to happen. The garage door was opening slowly and she was trapped. She wanted to reach for her thirty-two revolver, but the peaceful look of her daughter sleeping and her unsuspecting little boy in the back seat playing the game made her pause. She knew she had to do something and fast. She dialed Jam's number as the car whipped up behind her and two of the three dudes jumped out masked up.

One of the dudes was carrying an assault rifle while the other one had a big hand gun. The one with the handgun entered the passenger side of the car and had his gun aimed at their daughter. The one with the riffle was ready to spray the whole damn car up like he had a bottle of Raid and they were all roaches. Playing it safe, Tarnasha unlocked the doors.

On the other line, Jam was listening to the whole ordeal unfold, and it had his head all twisted up. He turned and whispered to Power-Up.

"Niggas robbing my wife," he said. A-K slid up in the back seat trying to hear what was going on. Jam heard the dude ask his wife where he was. He knew then it was more than a plain robbery. They wanted more.

"Call the white hoes," Jam said to Power-Up who quickly dialed the white girls.

"Helllooo," one of the white girls answered when she picked up the phone.

"What to tell 'em?" Power-Up asked Jam.

"Tell them we're going to speed up because of an emergency, but for them to keep calm and remain driving at the same speed," Jam explained. Power-Up related the message to the white girls.

"They said aight," Power-Up said back to Jam.

"Tell 'em to take the car back to the house in Zachary, get their own car, and I'll catch up with them later," Jam said still listening at what was going on with his wife and kids.

Tarnasha's mind started doing back flips realizing that she and her kids were cornered. She was feeling like it wouldn't be so bad if the kids weren't with her. Ty looked up from playing his game and just stared from one gunman to the next. The gunman on Tarnasha's side opened the door and demanded for her to step out the car.

"I'm not leaving without my kids," she said thinking they was bout to make her get in the car with the third man who was behind the wheel with a mask on. The gunman on the passenger's side tucked his gun away then picked the little girl up who never awoke from sleeping. Ty opened the car door himself, stepped out, and ran around to where his mother were standing.

"In there," the gunman said to Tarnasha pointing his riffle toward the open car garage. She left her phone on the console hoping Jam was listening.

"You have an alarm?" The gunman holding her daughter asked.

"Yes," she answered.

"Disconnect it, and do it right. Anything shady and I'll kill you and the kids," the gunman with the rifle said. Tarnasha disconnected the alarm system, and then the gunman placed her and the kids in one room. Boo got the assault rifle from Seven and handed him his tool. He whispered and told him to get Bouncy. Seven tore up outside, jumped behind the wheels of Tarnasha's car, and sped off to pick up Bouncy. Buck was following behind him in the renter.

"Can I join you?" Juicy asked when she made it inside the VIP section where YoungOne was chillin and sippin on some Grey Goose.

"Why not," YoungOne said smiling. He knew she was going to find him.

"I'm Juicy," she said introducing herself.

"I see the name on ya ass," YoungOne stated with a smirk on his face.

"Which one are you?" she asked.

"Whatcha mean?" YoungOne asked without answering her question.

"I see that chain and only one other person comes in here with one," Juicy said.

"I'm YoungOne," he answered.

"It's four of y'all right?" Juicy asked.

"That's it," YoungOne said.

"Where's Power-Up at? I haven't seen him in bout a week and a half," she continued.

"Out of town," YoungOne stated. He was about to ask Juicy how he could get some of her, but his phone started vibrating on his side.

"What's up, Thug?" YoungOne answered. Seeing Jam's number, YoungOne thought he was calling to make sure he was laying low.

"Man, listen! Something just happened with my wife and kids," Jam said in a panicked tone.

"Whatcha talkin bout?" YoungOne asked. Jam went on to tell him about Tarnasha calling not saying anything and what all he heard in the background. When Jam finished running it, YoungOne jumped up and said, "I'm on my way over there right now!"

"NO! You can't do it like dat. That's too risky for my kids," Jam said.

"What you want me to do then?" YoungOne asked looking at Juicy sitting across in front of him.

"Get a handgun with the silencer and a choppa. But, you gonna need somebody to drop you off on the back street. Then jump the fence and come up in my back yard," Jam explained.

"I'm on my way, Thug," YoungOne replied.

"Protect my family, Thug," Jam responded in a worried voice, feeling helpless at the same time.

"I gotcha my nigga," YoungOne said trying to give Jam hope.

"Call me back as soon as you make it in my back yard," Jam said.

"Aight. Ask Power-Up if I can trust Juicy?" YoungOne stated.

"Who is dat?" Jam asked without replaying the message.

"Just ask Power-Up and he'll explain," YoungOne said demandingly. Jam turned to Power-Up and asked him the question.

"Power-Up said she's a real Gutta Girl," Jam told YoungOne then asked him why.

"Because I'm at the strip club that Power-Up be going to all the time, and I'm sitting here with her. That's who I'ma use to drop me off," YoungOne explained.

"Fa show, one," Jam said.

"One," YoungOne responded back then hung up. Juicy had been listening to everything YoungOne was saying and asking on the phone. She knew something happened. She just couldn't put it all together. YoungOne explained what happen and what he needed her to do. She went in the back, grabbed her purse and followed YoungOne to his car.

Jam had placed his phone on mute in case the nigga or niggaz decided to pick up his wife's phone. He was still listening while he talked to YoungOne on his Black Berry phone. Shit had got quiet for some time then he heard a car door shut and the car start up. Jam figured that his wife had left her phone in the car. Jam was thinking to himself while Power-Up and A-K was sitting there with worried looks on their faces.

"Whoever was driving the car must be alone because they not saying a thing," Jam said out loud.

"Whatcha talking bout?" Power-Up asked. Jam explained that he think Tarnasha left her phone in the car when everything went down. He heard the car door close again even though he thought somebody was driving it.

"What's up?" The voice said. Jam's heart started beating fast because he thought the voice was asking him the question. Then he heard another voice saying that shit went smooth.

"How the bitch was acting?" Jam heard the first voice ask. Jam wanted to place the phone up to Power-Up and A-K's ears to see if they recognized the voices but didn't because he didn't want to miss the conversation the niggaz were having.

"It was one nigga in the car at first but he just picked up another person," Jam said out loud for Power-Up and A-K to hear him.

"She ain't trip. Bitch didn't even say nothing when we tied her and the lil boy up," the first voice said. Jam concluded that the first voice was the driver.

"Where the lil girl at?" the passanger nigga asked.

"She never woke up from sleeping. I just laid her down on the sofa," the driver said.

"This fucking nigga need to hurry up and come home," the voice said.

"Huh bra," the passenger replied in agreement.

"I might kill that fool," the driver stated.

Jam's palms started sweating and beads of sweat were visible all over his face.

"This a nice ass Gucci bag. Let me see what's in it," the passenger said. Jam could hear the nigga pouring all the stuff out the bag and wondered if his wife had her strap, but that thought was quickly put to rest when he heard one of the nigga say:

"Bitch got a lil snug-nose thirty-two."

Jam then heard a door close and a nigga quoting one of Lil Boosie songs 'Big money, I like it.'

"What it do my nigga?" The strange voice said.

"They just picked up another nigga," Jam said out loud but to no one in particular.

"This the hoe phone?" The new voice asked. "This bitch gotta iPhone," the voice continued but then the phone went dead in Jam's ear.

Tanarsha was sitting on the sofa with Ty right next to her while her daughter was sound asleep. She started talking to the masked gunman standing before her, who couldn't seem to keep still.

"Whatcha want?" She asked looking at the gunman who had his back to her as he looked out the window.

"I want yo husband to come home and cooperate," the gunman stated.

"I promise you he will, just let us leave," Tanarsha replied.

The gunman walked to the window and peeked out the curtains and saw Tanarsha's car pulling up.

Seven pulled the car in the garage then he, Buck, and Bouncy entered the house to search it as they waited on Jam to arrive.

"What time can we be expecting yo man," Seven asked soon as they made it in the room where Boo nem was.

"I don't know, but it'll be later on tonight," Tanarsha concluded.

"You might be dead by then or one of them," Seven said looking at the kids with an evil smirk on his face.

"Chill with dat shit," Boo said looking at Seven.

Buck walked over to where Tanarsha was and raised her nurse's skirt up to take a peek at what kind of underwear she had on. Ty jumped up when Buck did dat and just stared angrily at him.

"Search the house," Boo stated trying to give his clique something to do until Jam showed up. He figured he needed to keep them busy before one of 'em did some dumb shit. Just then, the cordless phone on the wall started ringing.

Trying not to crack under pressure, YoungOne drove home and changed into all black. He already had one of his straps on his side, but he rushed in and got his 45 with the silencer on it, grabbed the choppa from under his bed, and quickly made it back to the car where Juicy was waiting.

YoungOne got into the car then he and Juicy zoomed through traffic trying to make it to Jam's house while also making sure they were careful not to get stopped by the police. They pulled up on a street behind Jam's house and stopped the car.

"Keep my car; I know where to find you," YoungOne said to Juicy then eased out of the car. He looked back at Juicy climbing over getting in the driver seat and read her lips mouthing the words "be careful."

YoungOne disappeared between two brick houses.

CHAPTER EIGHTEEN

A million and one things were going through his head and not having the answers to none of them drove Jam crazy. He dialed his house number and the phone was just ringing.

He was about to hang up but didn't want to because of fear he'd felt for his family.

"Hello," answered his wife's trembling voice.

"Hey, baby," Jam said wanting to tell his wife he knew exactly what was up.

"Just getting in," Tanarsha replied.

"Where my babies?" Jam asked.

"You already know Tyesha's sleep. Ty's still playing the 'game boy," Tanarsha responded.

"I tried to call your cell phone but you ain't picked up," Jam said trying to let her know he heard what went down.

"Oh, I forgot it in my car," Tanarsha said hoping at the same time he heard what happened to his wife and kids.

"Oh, dats why I called the house phone," Jam responded then heard his lil girl crying in the background.

YoungOne set the guns under the house a little then crept on side of the house trying to see inside. All of the curtains were pulled together tightly, making it hard to see inside. He eased back to the backyard because he didn't want the neighbors to see him and call the police. He almost forgot to call Jam just that quick. He went and got the choppa back from under the house and sat on a bucket that was nearby while he dialed Jam's number. He didn't get an answer, so he called Power-Up's phone.

"What's up Thug?" Power-Up answered.

"Shit. Where's Jam at?" YoungOne asked.

"He's on the phone with Tanarsha," Power-Up said.

"Ask him what's up?" YoungOne stated.

"I'll ask him when he hangs up with her," Power-Up replied.

"Y'all know how many niggaz it is?" YoungOne asked.

"Jam said he thinks it's four of them," Power-Up continued.

"I wonder who these clowns are," YoungOne stated.

"I don't know, but they some dead niggaz," Power-Up said.

"What Tanarsha saying?" YoungOne asked.

"Really nothing," Power-Up answered.

"You think we know 'em?" YoungOne asked.

"I hope not because nigga must feed the fish with them." Power-Up replied.

"For real," YoungOne replied and then he told Power-Up to hold on. "Sounds like somebody throwing shit around."

Tyesha had finally woke up and the sight of seeing her mama and brother tied up with some strange man standing over them with a mask while pointing a gun at her mama's head as she was talking on the phone, made Tyesha start crying hysterically. The gunman then whispered in Tanarsha's ear for her to hang up the phone.

"What my baby crying for?" Jam asked.

"I gotta go see what's wrong with her, call back," Tanarsha said before hanging the phone up in his ear.

Jam looked over at Power-Up. "They made her hang the phone up," he explained.

"Well, YoungOne said hold on also. He said it sounded like somebody was throwing shit around," Power-Up told Jam as he handed him the phone. Jam held the phone to his ear for some time before YoungOne came back to the phone.

"Power-Up," YoungOne called out when he put the phone back to his ear.

"This Jam."

"I heard noise in one of the rooms but I can't see in none of 'em," YoungOne replied.

"Just keep watching. We should be there in bout another hour and forty-five minutes," Jam stated.

"What you gonna do then?" YoungOne asked.

"This the plan. Y'all hear me?" Jam asked to YoungOne, Power-Up, and A-K. Power-Up leaned over, and A-K scooted up so he could hear.

"Once we make it to Baton Rouge, I'ma go to my house in Clinton for A-K and Power-Up can get their tools. Then I'ma drop them off on the back street so they can come where you at," Jam explained to his clique. "Power-Up gonna have the back door keys. Once y'all see me pull up, I'ma wait for a few minutes. That's gonna give y'all enough time to come through the back then I'ma go inside where the niggaz waiting," Jam concluded.

"I'm dumping my whole clip in anyone of 'em I get first," A-K said acting like he had a gun in his hand.

"Sounds like a winner," Power-Up stated.

"I need two of y'all in the master bedroom because dats where I'ma lead 'em to," Jam replied.

"Me and Power-Up gonna be in there," A-K said.

"YoungOne, A-K, and Power-Up gonna be waiting in the bedroom. You be in the closet right in front dat room," Jam concluded

"Aight," YoungOne said.

"Stay laying low. I'ma hitcha back when we make it back to Baton Rouge but call me if anything happens," Jam stated.

"Fa show, one," YoungOne replied.

"One," Jam said before hanging up.

Talking to her husband eased her mind a little bit, and Tanarsha had a strong feeling that Jam knew what was going down. Her thoughts were interrupted when the masked gunman started talking.

"Don't seem like yo man coming home anytime soon," the masked gunman said.

"He'll be home later," Tanarsha stated.

"We got all night to wait," the gunman responded looking at her hard under his mask.

"Whatcha want?" Tanarsha asked trying to get him to stop looking at her like dat.

"I told you what I wanted," the masked gunman stated.

"When you get my husband then what?" she asked.

"This ain't about Jam," the gunman replied. When Tyesha heard her daddy's name come from the masked gunman's mouth, she removed her head from off her mama's lap and looked up at him.

"Well, what or who this about?" Tanarsha asked after placing her daughter head back on her lap.

"All I want is a lot of money or a lot of work," the masked gunman said.

When Ty heard the gunman the word "money," he thought about his savings of $120 that he kept under his mattress and hoped the gunman didn't take it. Tyesha started crying again only this time she could barely be heard with the tape around her mouth.

"It's gonna be alright baby," Tanarsha whispered in her daughter's ear.

The gunman turned around from looking out the window. He was about to say something to Tanarsha until one of the other masked men walked in the room.

"Why you looking at me?" he asked looking at Jam's son. Ty couldn't say anything because of the duct tape around his mouth, so he just stared at the gunman.

"Which one we waiting on?" the gunman asked walking up on the other gunman while holding up a nice sized picture in a frame. The gunman looked at the picture and saw how the four niggaz was shining on it. He pointed to a nigga with a cocky frame smiling and showing all ten of his gold teeth.

"Aight, dats Jam. I never been up close on him before. Now who the other ones is?" The gunman asked while still holding the picture.

"This one is A-K," the gunman said pointing at a slim built nigga, smiling showing every platinum and diamond in his grill. Then he pointed to a lil slim red nigga who was showing his twelve platinums saying dat was YoungOne.

"And so this is Power-Up?" the gunman asked looking at the last nigga on the picture who had a lil smirk on his face grilling the camera down and grabbing his crushed out 'Gutta Boy' chain on his neck.

"Dude need to hurry the fuck home," the gunman said then dropped the picture and walked off to go finish searching the house. Tanarsha and her kids were staring at the picture for different reasons. The kids wished their daddy and his boys were there because they felt everything would be ok. Tanarsha was staring at the picture thinking should she be blaming Jam for the predicament her and the kids were in. Seeing all of them looking at the picture on the floor made the gunman mad. The masked gunman stomped the picture until the frame broke. Then he picked up the picture and tore it up.

"You must hate my husband?" Tanarsha asked not knowing what response to expect back.

"I told you, this not about yo husband," the gunman said walking off to look out the window. Tanarsha started talking but he didn't hear her because the shadow he'd just seen had his full attention.

YoungOne was sitting on the bucket bored and tweaking for some action but not wanting to cause any harm for his dawg's wife and kids. He tried again to look through a few windows. He crawled damn near all the way to the front of the house when he saw the side window to the living room curtain barely open. YoungOne raised up to take a peek, but before he could look through, he saw a ski masked man coming into view. He quickly ducked down and crawled under the house, hoping he didn't get spotted. He was sliding on his arms and stomach to the back of the house. The phone started vibrating on his side, spooking him.

"What's up?" YoungOne whispered lying flat on his stomach.

"Shit still the same?" Jam asked.

"Yeah, nothing moving. I don't even hear them no more," YoungOne replied. He didn't tell Jam that he'd almost been spotted by one of the gunman.

"We should be there in thirty minutes," Jam stated.

"Aight," YoungOne said.

"I'll hitcha back when we make it to the back street behind my house," Jam concluded.

"Fa show," YoungOne replied.

"Make sure you call me if shit change," Jam said.

"You already know," YoungOne said.

"Aight, one," Jam responded.

"One," YoungOne said back then hung up the phone started snake maneuvering on his belly heading towards the back of the house.

Inside, the masked man moved to different windows to see if he could spot anybody.

He'd seen a flag on the neighbor's house about twenty feet away and convinced himself that *that* was what he saw.

"You heard what I said?" Tanarsha asked the gunman, seeing a string of paranoia for a moment on his face.

"I wasn't listening," the gunman stated.

"I'm trying to be helpful," she replied.

"Only way you can be helpful to me is if you know where the work or a whole lot of bread, is at" the masked man said.

"I can give you some money," Tanarsha said trying to see where the gunman's head was.

"Bitch, can't you see I'm here to get paid. I don't want pocket change!" the gunman replied angrily.

"You said this wasn't bout my husband so who this about?" Tanarsha responded.

"You starting to talk too much," the gunman said looking at her with the same strange look from earlier. Tanarsha, not wanting to piss the gunman off, closed her mouth and put her head down to kiss her daughter.

One of the other masked men walked in the room holding a box full of jewelry. Another one pulled a knot of money out his pocket and said, "I think we are on to something."

The biggest of the clique walked in the room eating a big sandwich he'd fixed himself. He then walked over to Tanarsha and put the sandwich to her mouth asking her if she wanted a piece. She just stared at him without answering.

"You act like you mad," the masked man stated with his gun stuck in the front of his pants. Tanarsha wished she could take the gun and blow his brains out.

"I want you to eat," he said trying to force the sandwich in her mouth.

She closed her mouth tightly and moved her head from side to side. The masked gunman tired of the sandwich and playing with Tanarsha, slapped her across the head with the sandwich.

"What the fuck you doing?" The gunman asked the gunman who was standing at the window.

"Fuck dat hoe," the gunman said laughing.

"We ain't come here for no dumb shit. Now y'all chill with the bull shit. If dude don't act right then it's whatever," the gunman replied moving away from the window.

CHAPTER NINETEEN

J am pulled up in front his house in Clinton and right on
point A-K and Power-Up were up out the car walking towards the front door. Jam moved quickly to the door then
unlocked it. They all rushed to the room where the guns
were. A-K grabbed two forty-fives and a silencer. Power-Up
settled for a Glock-40 and a Glock-9 with a silencer. Jam, felt
he didn't need a tool because he was the bait, and didn't
have the time to change into an all-black get-up. They all
rushed back to the car and headed towards Jam's wife and
kids for the takedown and the rescue.

"Man its 10:45. This nigga better hurry up because his
wife turning me on," said the masked man who'd looked
under Tanarsha's skirt earlier.

"I agree with dat," a different gunman said getting
up off the sofa and walking into another room. Tanarsha
looked up at the gunman standing back by the window trying to get him to show sympathy towards her in case one of

the other masked men tried something before her husband made it home.

YoungOne made it back to the bucket and took a seat. But, being anxious and not knowing what was about to take place when his boys made it, had him unable to keep still. He eased on a different side of the house trying to see if he could get a look inside. He remembered almost being spotted by the masked man on the inside of the house before, so he concluded it be best if he made his way back to the bucket to sit down. He picked up the choppa off the ground and began pointing it throughout the backyard. He heard noises that seemed close to him, so he stooped down, pointing the gun out in front of him trying to figure out where the noise came from. Just then, he saw the back door opening up. Quickly, he disappeared off the bucket and then slid up under the house. He was lying underneath the house, and his heart was beating so fast and loudly that he swore it could be heard by the masked gunman. Then, he heard the door close. He decided to stay where he was until Jam call him.

The closer they got the house, the more nervous Jam was becoming—not from being scared or anything, but from not knowing what might happen to his family. Everything was quiet in the car. All three of 'em were in their own little worlds.

"Man, I can't believe this shit's happen," A-K stated bringing Jam and Power-Up out of their zones.

"Me neither, thug," Power-Up responded. Jam just shook his head from left to right then grabbed the phone to call YoungOne to let him know they were pulling up on the back street.

"What up?" YoungOne answered.

"Power-Up and A-K'll be heading your way in bout three minutes," Jam said.

"Aight," YoungOne replied.

"Much luv, see you inside," Jam responded.

"Much luv," YoungOne said back then hung up the phone.

Jam stopped his car and looked at Power-Up and A-K then spoke, "let's do the damn thang."

A-K gave Jam pound and started getting out the car. Power-Up did the same and then he and A-K dashed between the brick houses.

Jam pulled off with many thoughts racing through his mind. He turned the corner making a right turn then cruised down Greenwell Street. Jam wanted so badly to hit everything on the dash board to get home faster. Even though he was about a hundred yards away from his crib, he played it cool because he didn't wanna alarm the stick up niggaz. He pulled in the drive way and fumbled around in the glove compartment box trying to stall time for his boys to make their move.

YoungOne rolled from under the house and sat back on the bucket when he saw Power-Up and A-K coming from between the two brick houses then entering into Jam's back yard. He felt a whole lot of stress come off his shoulders because now he had his dawgs to handle business with on the niggaz inside.

"What's up, Thug?" A-K asked giving YoungOne pound.

"Ready to dump in a nigga dome," YoungOne replied.

"What's up, nigga?" Power-Up greeted holding his two glocks, one in each hand.

"Good now," YoungOne responded.

Power-Up stuck one of the glocks in the front of his pants and one in the back. He pulled the keys out of his pockets Jam gave him for the door. He walked up to the burglar-bar door and slid the key in.

"Wait 'til Jam pull up because a nigga just opened dat door," YoungOne stated. As soon as Power-Up slid the key out the door, Jam turned in the driveway.

The masked man who never left Tanarsha and the kids' side was about to go take a leak. He peeped out the window and saw car lights, so he backed up a little from the window being cautious in case it was Jam's car. To his surprise, the car pulled into the drive way. The gunman turned and pointed to one of the other gunman and said, "I don't know if this dude, but a car just pulled up." He really couldn't see inside the car because it was dark.

"Get ready just in case it's him," the gunman said straining his eyes trying to see inside the car. One of the other masked men ducked down and went to find the gunman who left out the room earlier.

The gunman recalled that he'd never seen the car outside in the yard before when he used to stalk the house previously. He expected to see one of Jam's personal whips. The lights inside the car came on, and it was then that he saw Jam.

"It's him," the gunman said. By this time, the other gunmen had made it back to the front of the house and were standing close by the front door. Tanarsha was happy that Jam had made it home, but she was also feeling worried.

"He getting out the car," the gunman said as he checked his gun to make sure one was in the chamber. The other three gunmen checked their guns also.

"Jam just pulled in," A-K said.

"Let's get it," YoungOne replied.

Power-Up slid the key back in the burglar-bar door then opened the door that led to the kitchen. Power-Up pulled the door back slowly. He waited a few seconds to see if anybody was in sight. After the coast was clear, he, A-K and YoungOne moved in with their guns loaded and cocked. They were creeping like cats when they heard the sound of footsteps. They stopped in their tracks, and as soon as the footsteps could be heard fading away, they continued to their destination. When they made it to the master bedroom door, Power-Up told the crew to hold up a moment. Then, he tiptoed down the hallway and lied down on the carpet floor. He looked around the corner in the living room. "Fuck yeah," he thought to his self because he realized he had the upper hand on all four of the niggaz who had their backs turned.

Tanarsha was sitting there tied up with her daughter lying on her lap while Ty was next to her also tied up. Power-Up felt like he, A-K and YoungOne could shoot the niggaz down right where they were standing since their attention was on Jam who was still outside in the car. He looked back and was about to beckon for A-K and YoungOne when he heard the front door open and one of the niggaz yelling "Bitch don't move!"

All he could do then was rush to the bedroom and wait. YoungOne ducked off in the closet and put a small crack in the door like Jam said to do.

Jam came through the front door and was greeted with four guns drawn on him. One of the gunmen, who was standing next to the door, slammed the door shut and handed his pistol to one of his boys.

"Lay the fuck down!" the gunman in control said. Jam did as he was told, but he never took his eyes off his wife and kids.

"Don't do this in front my kids," Jam replied.

"Nigga fuck yo kids," the masked man said who gave his gun up. He now had duct tape in his hands. He walked over to Jam and kicked him in the side then searched him down. Seeing that Jam wasn't strapped, the masked man began to tie him up. The biggest masked man of 'em reached his tool to the gunman who was next to him.

"Stand the fuck up!" he yelled to Jam after giving his gun up.

"What y'all want?" Jam asked after the big masked man threw him on the sofa.

After throwing Jam on the sofa across from his wife and kids both of the masked men received their guns back.

"Bitch ass nigga you don't ask questions, you answer them," one of the gunman said.

"Now listen. I'ma ask you one time and one time only. You play games, my dawgs gonna rape your wife then kill her and them pretty kids of yours," threatened the gunman who Jam understood was running shit.

"What's up?" Jam asked.

"Fake ass nigga didn't I tell you don't ask question," the gunman said back-handing Jam in the face. The biggest masked man grabbed Jam's daughter off Tanarsha's lap and put his gun to her head.

"Where the dope at?" the gunman in charge asked.

"I don't have none here," Jam replied staring at his daughter crying hard.

"Nigga you better have something here," the gunman stated holding Jam's little girl tighter.

"All I have is money here," Jam responded.

"How much," one of the gunman asked.

"Close to three hundred grand," Jam replied. All four of the gunmen looked at each other with smiles on their faces.

"Where it's at?" asked one of the gunman.

"In my room, in the safe," Jam answered.

"Man, we checked every fucking room in this house and didn't see no safe," the gunman said still holding Tyesha by her shirt.

"It's under the bed," Jam stated.

"Get up!" the masked man in charge demanded. Jam stood to his feet and tried to kiss his daughter, but the gunman standing behind him kicked him in the butt. Being that his legs were taped together, Jam stumbled and fell face first on the plush pink carpet. The masked man dropped Tyesha on the floor and went to pick Jam up so he could lead them to the money.

Power-Up and A-K was standing in a closet full of Tanarsha's clothes. They both had tucked the guns without the silencer in their pants and had the ones with the silencer in their hands. Power-Up stepped out the closet and walked to the bedroom door attempting to hear or see anything. YoungOne, seeing Power-Up peeping, decided to stick his head out the closet, too.

"What's up?" he asked in a whisper.

"Ready to pop a nigga top" Power-Up responded back.

"Huh bra," YoungOne replied.

"Sound like they coming," Power-Up stated then hurried back to him and A-K's hide out. YoungOne got back in position and listened to the voices, which were getting closer and closer.

"See if you stunting, I'ma take it out on dat lil sweet daughter of yours," the big gunman replied holding Jam by the collar of his shirt. The four masked men and Jam were in the hallway leading towards the bathroom.

"Stay in there with them, the head gunman said to the masked man who been making sexual gestures toward Tanarsha from the moment he made it to the home.

"Aight," the masked man said then turned around.

YoungOne was standing in the closet with the choppa in his right hand. He wanted to come out and start spraying all three of the robbers up, but that would put his main man Jam's life in jeopardy. He watched as the three gunmen led his dawg to the bed room. YoungOne leaned the choppa against the wall and pulled his forty-five desert eagle out his pants then made sure the silencer was secured on it. When they made it to the bedroom, Jam could tell the masked men had been in there searching.

"Where it's at?" asked the masked man holding Jam tightly.

"You have to move the bed," Jam responded. The gunman threw Jam to the floor and he and one of the other masked men moved the bed to the side. After moving the bed and not seeing the supposed-to-be safe, made the one calling the shots angrier than two pit bulls about to rumble. He aimed his sawed off at Jam.

"Nigga, you playing games?" he asked immediately staring Jam down.

"Nah, ya gotta move the carpet back," Jam replied.

The big masked man who Jam had built the most hatred towards outta all of them, placed his gun on the floor and started pulling the carpet back. Moments later, the top of the safe in the floor came into view.

"What's the combination?" The gunman calling the shots demanded.

"Eleven left, one right, and eight left," Jam answered.

The big masked man turned the numbers on the safe then looked at Jam when it didn't open.

"Ya gotta pull the latch up," Jam stated.

The masked man pulled the latch, and the safe door opened up. "Jackpot!" the gunman shouted out loud, looking at his boys. The other two masked men moved closer to see inside the safe.

"I told y'all this was the big come up!" The gunman in charge said in an excited voice. The big gunman placed his weapon on the floor and started pulling out stacks of money.

Power-Up and AK were waiting on the right time to take the three gunmen out. They were peering through a crack in the closet door.

"You see dat?" A-K asked talking about one of the masked men laying his gun down.

"Fuckin right," Power-Up replied.

Then the gunman who was doing most of the talking bent down on one knee, placed his sawed off on the floor, and joined his boy pulling money out the safe. He looked back at the masked man who was still holding his 357 revolver. "Find something to put this in!"

The masked man looked around the bedroom for something then he trotted over to the closet.

Jam was lying on the floor looking at the closet door, wondering whether his dawgs were in there or not. He knew the money would distract the robbers and it did. Now, it was on his dudes to handle the rest. Jam knew that if Power-Up and A-K were waiting in the closet then at any given moment, gunfire would start. To be on the safe side, Jam stayed glued to his snow white carpet. He heard the gunman in charge tell the masked man standing by his head to find something to put the money in. That command sent the gunman head first straight towards Power-Up and A-K. The masked man moved quickly to the closet and pulled the door open. Before he knew what happened A-K shot him straight in the head. Hearing the funny noise, the robbers turned around in disbelief and saw A-K and Power-Up running their way letting off shots. The masked men tried to pick up their guns but they knew they'd been caught with their pants down.

Power-Up had shot one of them three times and stopped dude instantly from trying to retrieve his gun. A-K dumped his whole clip in the other masked man then bent down to take off the masks he was wearing.

"It got one more," Jam said as Power-Up was taking the tape off his arms and legs.

A-K ran to the door and beckoned for YoungOne, who was hiding in the hallway closet, to come out. YoungOne was heated because he didn't get a chance to kill none of the gunmen.

"There's one more," A-K said to YoungOne who was feeling left out of the action.

"I wanna kill this one," YoungOne stated.

"We gotta get him in here," Jam replied.

"Come on," A-K said to YoungOne and walked to the hallway. He was looking at A-K confused.

"Be ready, I'ma get him back here," A-K concluded looking back at YoungOne.

A-K then crept halfway down the hallway and hollered, "Man, look at all this money!" Then, he ran to the closet where YoungOne was hiding out. He left the door open but not wide open. YoungOne was standing on side the bedroom door. Power-Up posted up on the other side. Jam grabbed the dead masked man sawed off and posted up behind Power-Up.

The masked man was still in the room with Tanarsha and the kids, and he was pacing the floor. Every now then he'd look into the hall way. Tanarsha was sitting there wondering what the hell was going on in her bedroom. She was saying a silent prayer that she didn't hear a gunshot. Then, she heard a voice that sounded like A-K's saying something about money. The masked man was making his way to look out the window when he thought he heard one of his boys say something. He rushed to the hall way, and not seeing anyone peaked his curiosity. The masked man started walking towards the bedroom where the door was open. He made it to the bedroom and saw two of his boys stretched out. It was too late for the gunman. A-K had his glock pointed at the back of dude's head

"Nigga don't move!" A-K demanded with his finger on the trigger. Then A-K, realized he had emptied his whole clip with the silencer on it in the other masked man's head and body. Shit, A-K thought to himself. He hoped the masked gunman didn't try no crazy shit. A-K called out

YounOne's name loud enough for him to hear. YoungOne came around the corner, screamed for A-K to move out of the way, and proceeded to dump eight shots in the masked man body. PowerUp went ahead and emptied what he had left in his clip with the silencer for good measure. The gunman was so shocked about what was happening that he forgot he even had a strap. The gunman stumbled backwards and slid down the wall with a tight grip on his forty-four revolver. Jam hauled tail to the front room to check on his wife and kids. A-K took the gun out the dead man's hand and snatched his mask off.

"Y'all know dat fool?" A-K asked dropping the ski mask on the floor walking off to the bedroom. Power-Up and YoungOne took a look at dude and followed A-K across the hall to the bedroom. A-K walked towards the dead man he had shot point blank range in the face. He took the mask off dude and said, "Don't know him neither." Then he walked to where the remaining two dead men lay.

He took the ski mask off the big dead man and said, "I can tell I don't know him,"

YoungOne and Power-Up looked at the dead man then moved their eyes towards A-K taking the last gunman's mask off. Dude had a hole in his head with several bullet holes in his body. He was laying there with his eyes wide open. Power-Up looked in the eyes of what used to be his main-man.

"I be a mutha fuck!" Power-Up yelled.

"I seen this nigga about a month ago leaving Keba's Beauty Shop," A-K replied.

"You know this fool?" YoungOne asked looking at Power-Up.

"Yep," Power-Up answered. They heard a loud grunt and looked at the man dying man who lay before them. "This a nigga named Boo," PowerUp concluded. Then, he walked towards the bed and got a pillow. He came back to the dying man and placed the pillow on his face smothering all the life out of dude. "I'll tell y'all bout him when we get rid of these bodies," Power-Up said then walked off to go see how Tanarsha and the kids were doing.

YoungOne and A-K checked the rest of the dudes to make sure all of 'em were dead.

Tanarsha was trying to take the tape off her hands when Jam ran in the living room. She started crying when she saw her husband, which led Tyesha to do the same. Ty just sat there smiling. As he was taking tape off his wife, Jam began explaining what had happened. He and Tanarsha removed the tape off their kids. Jam formed a group hug while Tanarsha said thank you prayers to the Lord.

Power-Up walked in the room and stood by the door until Jam and his kids came out their group hug. He then hugged Tanarsha and the kids. YoungOne and A-K made it to the living room and hugged Tanarsha and the kids, too.

"Take ya family and get outta here. We gonna take care of them niggaz," Power-Up said to Jam.

"Aight," Jam replied then dapped and hugged his boys.

Tanarsha and the kids hugged Power-Up, A-K, and YoungOne again and left with Jam to go to one of their other homes.

Power-Up, A-K and YoungOne tied the four dead niggaz in sheets like body bags. As they were cleaning the mess up, Power-Up told his dawgs about the history of him and Boo. A-K found the keys to Jam's Tahoe, which was parked in the garage. He pulled all the speakers out the back and then they piled the dead niggaz in the back. YoungOne and Power-Up followed A-K in Tanarsha's Lexus to the south where they dumped the bodies behind the levee in the bottom of the water. Once done, A-K called Jam to let him know everything had been taken care of and that it was all good.

It has been three months and two weeks since the kidnapping of Tanarsha and her kids. That same night, Jam retired out the game. Tanarsha and Jam moved to a new home on the outskirts of Baton Rouge in a country town.

A-K still being who he is, never changed his stripes.

Power-Up started taking heed to what niggaz said out their mouths since the Boo incident. Besides that, he never stopped hitting the strip clubs. He even considered opening one up himself.

YoungOne moved LaShay and her mama to a big and better house, so he didn't have to worry about DJ and his boys. Today was also YoungOne's nineteenth birthday, and he had been celebrating all day long. LaShay had given him a nice diamond ring, and later on, she was planning on given him her virgin pussy to conclude his birthday festivities.

The whole Gutta Boys family was in the club celebrating YoungOne's birthday. Every female worker from Keba's Salon were there. Several people from different shops The Gutta Boys owned was out showing love, too. Juicy and the twins were in the strip club shaking their asses. It was like a family reunion. Everybody in the club was drunk, high, or tipsy.

When the clock struck 3:30 in the morning, people started fading out. YoungOne went and found his boys to let 'em know he was about to roll. He thanked everyone from the DJ booth and let them know they could stay long as they wanted to but he was leaving the building. He was torn up. It was a good thing LaShay didn't drink. Even though she did take a few sips that night, she was still sober enough to drive.

YoungOne handed LaShay the keys to his drop top Benz that his dawgs went half on for his birthday. They jumped in the new whip and headed towards the main road.

LaShay was driving down Government Street when she stopped at the red light on the corner of 19th Street. YoungOne had his seat laid back enjoying the cool Baton Rouge breeze from the top being down on his Benz. LaShay looked in the rear view mirror at the blue Suburban coming up behind them. She didn't think anything of it until another dark-colored car pulled up around in front of them at the red light. The Suburban pulled up on side LaShay and YoungOne, and they were trapped. It seemed like everybody in it opened fire on them with machine guns in hand.

THE END

ABOUT THE AUTHOR

Bryan K. Johnson is a native of Plaquemine, Louisiana, who grew up in Baton Rouge. He has three brothers: Eric (a.k.a. "Baby face") Darryl, and Robert. At the tender age of eight in 1997 Johnson's sister, Darrilyn, was killed in an accident. Johnson was raised by his mother, Terry, and grandmother Carrie Mae "Bernard" Johnson.

Johnson has been incarcerated since the age of sixteen. He did not complete high school, but while incarcerated he received his GED and trained for various trades. Johnson has written five book manuscripts and two plays.

With his release date slowly approaching, Johnson trusts that God will see him home with his family: his mother, Terry; his son, Lil Bryan; his stepdaughters, Ty and Mia; and Shamecko, his devoted fiancé who continues to inspire him.

ORDER FORM

Boot Publishing Inc.

14785 Preston Rd Ste. 550

Dallas, TX 75254

Name:_____

Address:_____

City:_____ State:_____Zip:_____

Gutta Boyz   **$13.85**

By Bryan K. Johnson

Accepted forms of payment: Cashier Checks, Money Orders

**Mail payment to address above payable to: Boot
Publishing Inc.**

**For quick and easy method via PayPal, Credit Card for
online order**

Visit our website @ www: bootpublishing.com

Please allow 5-7 Business days for delivery.

- -